"We're protesting Trevor's suspension," Lorne said in a strong, controlled voice. "We believe it was unfair and that he should be allowed back."

Ryan was stunned. His silence caused mumbles of agreement to surface in several parts of the classroom.

"All right, that's enough," he said to no one person in particular. "Your behavior is foolish and immature. And pointless. You've been watching too much television."

"We're protesting for good reason," Lorne said.

Ryan looked at him. "Trevor was suspended with just cause. I have no intention of reversing that decision. Lorne, if you and the rest of the class don't give this up, you will be in serious danger of being given zeros on this test."

Some of the students, including Elaine, shifted about in their seats, exchanging anxious looks. Lorne waited, but nobody said anything. Eventually he spoke again. "Mr. Ryan, if we didn't believe you were wrong, we wouldn't be doing it."

KEVIN MAJOR is the author of several books for young readers, including *Far from Shore* and *Hold Fast*, available in Dell Laurel-Leaf editions. He lives in Newfoundland.

Thirty-six Exposures

Kevin Major

LAUREL-LEAF BOOKS bring together under a single imprint outstanding works of fiction and nonfiction particularly suitable for young adult readers, both in and out of the classroom. Charles F. Reasoner, Professor Emeritus of Children's Literature and Reading, New York University, is consultant to this series.

Published by
Dell Publishing
a division of
The Bantam Doubleday Dell Publishing Group, Inc.
666 Fifth Avenue
New York, New York 10103

ISBN: 0-440-20163-2

RL: 6.2

Reprinted by arrangement with Delacorte Press

Printed in the United States of America

September 1988

10 9 8 7 6 5 4 3 2 1

KRI

I am best photographed from a distance.
From there I could look average.
But as I come closer some   becomes apparent.
You would probably detect my   by the way
  I walk
and if I were to speak, a slight   might be
  noticed.
It's most likely, though, that I'd walk right past you
and not say a word.

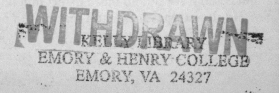

Two

Near the end of the climb he was forced to admit to himself that his Nikes were the wrong thing to have worn on his feet. His mother had been right—there were patches of ice still not melted. Several times his foothold had given way, scraping his ankles and sending rocks crashing down into the alder bushes below.

Once he slipped and the camera almost struck a rock. He caught himself on the ground with one hand, quickly pulling the camera in tight to his chest with the other. "Damn!" he blared. A sliver of rock had sliced the soft palm muscle below his thumb. When he stood up he spread the cut apart, sucking air through his teeth in pain. He pressed the flesh on either side of it but could force out no more than a thin line of blood.

He slowed his ascent, still making it a point not to look down. When he was safely over the top he moved far back from the edge and rested until his breathing calmed. Flattening out on his stomach in the rubbery growth of caribou moss, he guided himself slowly toward the full view.

It surpassed anything he had dared hope for. It would make an extraordinary photograph. The sweeping ridges of sea meeting a crescent of landwash crowded with wharves, sheds, fishing stages. Motorboats tight to their moorings off from shore. The modern expanse of the new fish plant. The houses—clapboarded white except for the recently built few with pastel siding—scattered on both sides of the only road. The narrow layer of asphalt winding from the plant, around the harbor to the intersection below him and the road leading to the Trans-Canada.

He worked a small pair of binoculars from one pocket and a portable radio from the other. He pinpointed the dial to the FM rock station. The relentless rhythms of The Who surged and faded with the gusting wind. He very carefully wedged the radio in the crack of the rock near him. Then with both hands he steadied the binoculars to his eyes, manipulating the focus with his index finger. A few lines came to him. He stored them away, with a reminder to write them down later.

> telescopic eyes strain at Marten
> my semicircular vision
> Cabot, Cook, Cartier, sailed by
> Beothuck Indians summered here
> four hundred years ago
> Englishmen came for cod, and stayed.

People living here centuries before most places in North America were even discovered. The names of those three explorers together, he proposed, would make a good name for a rock group. And what remained of the Beothucks? Their name on a campground for tourists, a sign showing a one-feathered cartoon character scampering about with a tomahawk.

He turned the binoculars seaward, through the narrow inlet of the harbor to the open ocean beyond. Sail straight across and you will strike France. Closer in distance than British Columbia. Someday, and not in the distant future at that, he knew he would trek the cities of Europe, the red maple leaf and the Newfoundland flag sewn side by side on a knapsack.

A boat turned in and around the point. He followed its course as it cleared the rocks and the shallows. He thought he recognized the two people but was sure only when the outboard cut and the boat slowed into the wharf. Trevor, a classmate of his, climbed out. Trevor's father tossed up the painter. They secured the boat, then transferred a knapsack and two guns to the wharf. Trevor set them aside. Then, lifting together each time, they landed their catch ashore—two harp seals, their gray-black markings clearly visible through the binoculars. He watched as they carefully slit the carcasses to get to the meat inside.

He started to picture himself as a son in that family. He stopped after a few seconds. Had he had a more powerful telescopic lens for his camera, he would have taken a photograph.

His sights shifted to the fish plant. Perhaps he would end up there like his father used to warn him. Working part of the year, drawing unemployment during the rest. Or Alberta. He had relatives living there now he could stay with. At least he would get to see a bit of the country. Maybe go to university like everyone expected, maybe not. That was no guarantee of a job anymore, especially with an arts degree when you were sure you didn't want to be a teacher. Train for a job with one of the oil rigs off the coast? After the Ocean Ranger disaster, he would never even mention that possibility to his mother. In any case, just two more months and he would be through, finished with high school. And in four more months he would be eighteen.

He drew back from the lookout and stood up in the wind. It whipped his hair in all directions. He unzippered his coat and spread it open like he used to do on Mercer's Bank when he was younger. He leaned forward, a human sail. Atop his world, he concluded; bloody dramatic.

Later, just before he left to go down, he made his way back to the edge. This time it was his camera that he held in his hands. It would definitely make a perfect opening shot for the history project—the sun low, the light he liked best. He held the camera in such a way as to avoid irritating the cut on his hand. He framed the scene and with certain purpose depressed the shutter.

Three

He reached the road as the streetlights came on. He looked at his watch. It displayed 8:42 in minute neon-red numerals. As he walked he considered the physics assignment due in on Monday. He'd work and get it done over the weekend, and on Monday morning for sure there'd be at least three people asking for it to copy. It was one of the things he hated most about high school.

The glare of high-beam headlights going past him disrupted his train of thought. The truck's tires locked and squealed for a second, then jerked in reverse and moved backward until the driver's door was alongside him.

It was Gwen in her father's pickup. She kept it moving backward in time with his walking. Her window was wide open.

"Lorne," she said, "I'm going back your way."

"That's okay."

He smiled, his brief smile that attempted to dispel any notion that he could be shy. She brought the pickup to a quick stop.

"You get off on walking?" she said, louder.

He walked on, ignoring the comment. She backed up far enough this time that he was forced to walk through the full beam of the headlights. She stopped the pickup again and tapped the horn.

He decided he couldn't face the consequences of going past her a second time. He turned and crossed in front of the truck to get to the passenger door. He opened it, climbed aboard, and closed himself inside.

He could feel that the seat was worn in places to the foam. As the pickup moved forward again an empty drink bottle rattled over the floor. Gwen took a cigarette from a pack and held it toward him.

"I keep forgetting," she said, and put it in her own mouth before he had a chance to refuse. "So when is the next meeting?"

"Monday."

"Good. I'd like to have more to do, you know. Ryan is going to start getting the idea that two or three people are doing all the work."

She waited for him to agree with her. He was thinking more about the fact that she still hadn't turned the pickup around. They were heading away from the house, along the stretch of road between Marten and Spencer's.

"You're not in a hurry."

"I've got to be home pretty soon."

After he said it he figured it sounded pretty lame. Timid.

"It's Friday night," she said.

What else was worth saying? He kept quiet. Farther up the road she flicked on a signal light.

She cut the steering wheel quickly to the right. The truck almost bottomed out because of a sudden dip in the road. It banged ahead over the gravel, splashing water out of the many potholes.

Eventually they broke out into an open field. Without warning she drove the gas pedal to the floor, spinning the tires wildly through the wet grass. He held on. His hand searched down and gripped the under edge of the seat. Cutting the wheels, she forced the truck sideways, first to the left, then just as sharply in the opposite direction.

He held silent. In sight of the pond she snapped her foot to the brake and came to a long, sliding stop. The headlights shone out over the water.

He quickly unlocked his grip and slid his hand back to his lap. She put the truck in neutral and leaned over the steering wheel.

She looked across at him with a grin that toyed with laughter. "There's a beaver's dam, so there must be beavers around. You said it'd be good to have a few shots of wildlife."

She couldn't be serious. "For sure the noise frightened them," he said, trying not to sound conned, in case it was meant to be a joke.

She shut off the headlights and turned the key in the ignition. "All right, you're the expert."

She took a final draw of the cigarette and twisted it out in the ashtray. She turned his way again. "How much is that thing worth?" she asked. She meant the camera that still hung around his neck.

"A few hundred dollars."

"Your old man must be loaded."

"Not quite," he said with abbreviated laughter.

A pine deodorizer swung erratically from the mirror. The sky had not yet reached the darkness of night, so any movement he made would be noticed. He longed for the comfort of hidden reactions.

"You're not scared of me?"

He laughed longer this time. "No."

She moved toward him. He tried to deny the tightening of his stomach muscles, the sudden unevenness in his pulse.

"Don't you find it a bit cold?" she asked.

"A bit." She had to be staring at him.

"I didn't think you'd be this nervous."

She passed her right arm along the top of the seat and held her hand against his neck. The cold touch caused him to flinch. He turned to her quickly and smiled to erase that reaction. Rather than have to stare at her, he moved his lips to meet hers. His arms encircled her loosely.

Now her fingers held his zipper and began to work it slowly open over the ridges of his jeans. She inched her fingertips past the metal edges to the inside. With all his mind he urged it to be getting hard.

She pressed her lips harder against his, at the same time rubbing her fingers into the strands of hair nearest the waistband of his underwear. Her tongue found a way between the tenseness of his lips. Her whole body suddenly urged forward.

"Ouch!" she blurted into his face. She sank back on

the seat, rubbing her breast with her retrieved hand. "That goddamn camera."

He straightened up. He zippered his jeans while she was occupied with her pain. A few seconds later he told her that probably it would be better if she did take him home.

Four

It was the first of two school dances in May, the final ones before the year-end exams. He danced twice and spent the rest of the time standing near two or three others in front of the stage listening to the band. He soon grew tired of their music. They weren't very good; they had neither the equipment nor the talent to do a good job on most of the songs they attempted. Once he'd decided to leave, he waited for them to play something loud so that even if anyone bothered to ask him where he was going, he could pretend not to hear.

Out in the corridor he saw Trevor standing by himself near the girls' washroom. He looked to be waiting for his girlfriend.

"Why the rush?" Trevor asked him.

He stopped. "Too hot in there for me."

"Not only that, the band is the absolute shits. Listen,

I'll be out in a few minutes. I've got a coupla beers in the car."

He allowed enough time to pass to give the impression that he was seriously considering it. "Thanks anyway," he said, and continued toward the side exit door.

He banged down hard and noisily on the bar lever and left.

Scrambling down the concrete steps, he turned toward the road. He walked along the edge of the pavement. A car passed, one headlight much dimmer than the other, its stereo blaring. He hoped nobody from school was aboard.

Midway between two streetlights he started to slow down. He finally stopped. Enough. He crossed the road and headed back in the direction he had come. The same car sped past him, blowing its horn loud and long.

But at the end of the school parking lot he found Trevor's car empty. He leaned his back against the passenger door, his hands in his jacket pockets. He waited.

He wondered why Trevor had bothered to offer him the beer. Probably it had something to do with them being on the project together. They had never been close friends through all the years they'd been in school. In some ways he envied Trevor—he always seemed to be having a better time.

When Trevor showed up he was with Barbara, his hand tight in hers. She was poking him as if he had just jokingly insulted her.

"Lorne, ay, right on," he said when he saw him. "Jump in."

Lorne opened the passenger door and climbed into the backseat. The front seat flipped back in place and Barbara sat next to Trevor.

"You get any good shots?" Barbara asked, looking over the seat.

"A few."

Trevor checked outside the car in all directions. Satisfied that there was nobody around, he reached under the front seat and came up with a beer. He laid it on the seat next to him. He stretched his arm down again and located a second one. With the metal end of the seat belt he snapped off the caps. The second one made a loud pop and deflected off the overhead light. He quickly covered the top with his mouth and sucked down what might have fizzed over. He handed the other over the seat.

"Here, lower that down."

Lorne took the beer and sat back in the center of the seat. The seat felt too wide for one person to get comfortable; the distance to the front seemed too great. He took a taste of beer. It went down cold and sharp, but he managed a second swallow right away.

Barbara shivered, rubbing her hands together as she held them between her knees.

"How about some heat?"

Trevor quickly enclosed her with his arms. "What part do you want warmed up?" They nestled in playful intimacy until she forced him away, almost causing him to spill the beer he held in his hand.

Lorne met his grin with one of his own and another gulp of beer. He offered a muted laugh.

"You look pretty down about something," Trevor said. "What's buggin ya?"

He shrugged. "Nothing."

"When I gets down, I finds the quicker I can get it back up again the better."

Trevor laughed, at the same time covering his head with his arm to block the open fist that Barbara aimed at him. Her hand glanced off his arm and caught the beer bottle, sending it smack against the dash and crashing to the floor.

Five

His mother was seated in the gliding rocker near the window, knitting the sleeve of a Mary Maxim sweater. The back part, patterned with a pair of Canada geese, was draped across the knitting basket next to her. She knitted and watched the last few minutes of *Dallas*. Through the sheer curtain she kept a glancing watch on the traffic passing on the road in front of the house.

His father lay asleep on the chesterfield, his face turned to the inside, a multicolored afghan covering him. On the coffee table was a tray with two china mugs and a half slice of toast. The toast was now cold, its coating of butter congealed.

Lorne closed the refrigerator door and walked into the living room, unwrapping the plastic from a slice of processed cheese. He stood in the middle of the room and watched as the TV program ended.

"You're home early," his mother said to him.

He didn't reply.

"You got a ride home?"

He hated it when she asked a question she already knew the answer to. He tried ignoring her again.

"Whose car was it?"

"What difference does it make?" he snapped.

She continued to knit. "When the sleeve is finished, your sweater'll be ready to sew together."

He took the half slice of cold toast from the tray and sat down.

"You don't have to eat that. I'll make you some more." She started to put her knitting to one side.

"Mom, sit down. If I want any I can get it myself."

The electronic music introducing the news caused her to alert her husband. "Frank, the news is on."

His father turned from his sleep and rose up on one elbow. "Did I sleep that long?" he said. "I got that policy to write up yet before I go to bed."

The broadcast opened abruptly with short clips of the major stories. Workers marching in Poland. Boys in Northern Ireland hurling rocks at soldiers. Protest in Ottawa and New York against nuclear armament. Lorne listened with intense interest.

"Remind me to give Cyril a call tomorrow about that town council meeting Tuesday night," his father said.

The announcer gave a detailed report of each item.

"Makes you realize just how lucky we are, living where we do," his mother commented.

"Don't be too sure," Lorne said. "We could be flattened in a nuclear war just as easy as anyone else."

"Don't go tellin your mother that. She worries

enough as it is. Next thing she'll be usin that as an excuse not to go."

"Sure, you go on to the Lions convention if you wants to go."

"It's only for a weekend, Blanche. He can look out to himself for that long. When I was his age I was left home for two years, working."

"What do you think I am—handicapped?" Lorne said to his mother.

"His grandmother'll keep an eye on him."

"I don't need Grandmother."

"Stella and Marion, they're both goin."

Lorne left them still in disagreement.

He went down the hallway to his room, closed the door, and locked it.

Six

Sometimes when he was alone something would trigger his thinking about what it meant for him to be alive. And that eventually he would be dead. The thought that there might be nothing else he could know about in the millions of years of time wrenched him in fright. It was absurd to now be so conscious yet to think that after he died there would be nothing of him forevermore. The thought made him jolt his head sideways and try to force his mind onto something else.

Unlocking the drawer of his desk, he took out a pen and his binder. He opened it to a clean sheet of paper.

> Headphones block, switched on rock
> Clash it out of your system
> Vibrating ears, forget your fears
> Live it like you mean it.

The single bed supports your head
A course for every reason
Posters squirm with no concern
Lennon, you are needed.

Darkened room, personal tomb
Incessant wants and urges
From magazines, girls beam
Leaving feelings unfielded.

But given a chance like he'd had, how many would
have wimped out that bad? Even if he didn't really like
her, it was a chance to friggin do it. How many millions
of people in the world are doing it right now? At any
time of the day or night how many are getting it?
Probably every split second, millions of rear ends
pumping away like mad.

All the muscles in his body stiffened in intense pleasure. He slipped the headphones off with his other
hand. A calming afterglow spread through his limbs. It
could have eased him into a gentle sleep but for the
strain of guilt he could never seem to root from his
mind. His brain countered with all the statistics he had
read. Nobody he knew ever admitted it, but a lot of
them had to be doing it just as often. And what difference did it make, anyway.

He straightened out in bed, propping his head up
farther with a second pillow. He leaned across his desk
and switched off the stereo. He knew for sure now that
he wouldn't sleep. Turning on the desk lamp, he an-
gled the shade toward his bed. The light gave him a
clear look at his thinness in the dresser mirror. He
studied his face, rubbing his fingers over it until they

came to rest on a reddish spot just below his lower lip. He squeezed the flesh together several times, until he felt pus between his thumb and forefinger.

He took the magazine and the binder and locked them both away in the drawer. Then, settled under the covers as comfortably as he could get, he opened the book of Yevtushenko's poetry that Langman had lent him and began to read.

Seven

He made a fractional adjustment to one of the tripod legs; then, bent over, he looked through the view-finder at the four of them again. No, it still wasn't exactly what he wanted. He moved the whole apparatus slightly to the right; he needed a better angle on the school in the background.

"You don't want to see more of that dump," Trevor said.

Lorne ignored the remark. "Okay," he told them, "now move closer together."

Trevor moved in front of Barbara, blocking her from view.

"Stop it," she said, her words partly smothered in his shoulder. "Trev, will you behave yourself."

"I'm tryin, I'm tryin. I had a hard night." He laughed. She glared at him in mock anger.

Lorne stood in back of the camera, still waiting. Gwen was on Trevor's right. Elaine on Barbara's left. The five of them formed the project group.

"Where are *you* going to stand?" Gwen asked him.

"I'll find a place," he said without looking directly at her.

He depressed the self-timer and darted out from behind the tripod to take a place with the others. Approaching them, he saw Gwen moving aside to open a space between her and Trevor. He ignored it and continued in the direction he had planned. He stood on the far right, next to Elaine, faced the camera, and smiled.

"Damn," he said, and moved out of line. "This is no good." He knew the positions were unbalanced. The shutter clicked. "Damn."

Back at the camera he advanced the film. He quickly came up with a compromise—alternating female and male, a logical balance. He ran to stand between Barbara and Elaine.

The picture would show Gwen on the far left, in jeans and jean jacket, more of her weight on one foot than the other, her arms hanging loosely. Then Trevor, curly-headed, in a kangaroo jacket, arms folded tightly, the trace of a grin breaking through his attempt to look deadly serious. Barbara, next to him, her blond hair woven into a braid, her hands in the pockets of her down-filled vest, only partly smiling. Lorne, hands behind his back, exposing more of his new sweater than he really wanted to, straight, thin, rigid. Elaine, on the far right, uncomfortably warm in a winter parka, her hands in the embroidered pockets holding it open, a shyness showing in her eyes.

After the shutter clicked, Elaine turned to Lorne and smiled. "We've got the first picture and the last," she said. "Now all we need is something to fill the space between."

"That shouldn't be hard," Lorne said confidently. "We know what we want."

"You know what *you* want," Gwen cut in. "I don't even think this is going to work. Ryan is looking for something written down on paper, not a bunch of pictures."

Lorne was taken aback. "There's going to be a lot more to it than that," he pointed out quietly. "There's the interviews and the narration."

"None of the other groups are doing it this way."

"We're being original. That's why we're going to get a better mark."

"I think we're taking too big a chance," Trevor said. "What if it ends up a flop? Some of us can't afford a low mark."

Barbara jumped at them. "Well, that's up to us, isn't it? If everyone isn't willing to work at it and do their share, then it *is* going to be a flop."

"I think we should go ahead and try it, at least," Elaine said.

Lorne smiled at her, pleased and a little surprised by the earnestness of her remark.

"Give it a chance, I s'pose," Trevor agreed finally. "It'll probably blow his mind."

"Or blow our marks," Gwen said.

Eight

Lorne and Elaine were the only people in the art room. Some noise filtered down from upstairs, a few people rushing out from after-school meetings, but, he conceded uneasily, nobody with any intention of coming down.

Intense fluorescent lights eliminated the normal basement gloom. At the rear a door led to the darkroom.

"The chemicals are all ready," Lorne told her as casually as he could. "I did that before you got here."

They were sitting across from each other at a small table, both of them looking sideways at a Kodak booklet on black-and-white enlarging. He concentrated on an explanation of the procedure that would take place in the darkroom. He kept it straightforward and technical. She nodded a lot and gave him the impression that she understood everything he said.

They moved inside then and closed the door. It seemed at first that they were cast in complete darkness. He thought it may have startled her.

"You have to give your eyes time to adjust," he said quickly.

The dull red glow from the ceiling light gradually lessened the darkness. Standing apart in silence, they discovered each other's features. He liked the chance it gave him to look at her for what could be another reason.

The enlarger, a line of three developing trays, the sink, all took shape. "Really," he stressed, "it isn't much of a darkroom. It has the essentials and nothing more. No timer, for one thing. Langman tried to get one, but the school wouldn't come up with the money.

"I use a watch, but after a while you get good at judging seconds," he continued almost in the same breath, "one one-thousandth, two one-thousandth. . . ." He stopped, thinking perhaps he had talked too long and stupidly.

The negative he chose to print was the one he had entered in the province-wide arts competition. He told her that as he was cleaning it of dust.

"When will you know if you won?"

"I don't expect to win. It's open to professionals too," he said, sorry that he had mentioned it.

He inserted the negative into the enlarger and pointed out to her the various adjustments needed to focus the exact size of image he wanted on the easel below.

"What is it?" she asked.

"You'll see."

"Who is that person?"

"My father." He made some adjustments to the easel so that the figure on the far right would be cut from the print. "But he gets cropped."

He inserted a #4 filter into the enlarger to add more contrast. "Now we switch off this light and get a sheet of paper." From a box in the drawer below he retrieved an 8 × 10 sheet. He fitted it under the edges of the easel, switched the enlarger light back on, and began counting out seconds. When he stopped, he cut the light.

He transferred the paper from the easel to the tray of Dektol. He submerged it image-side down with his fingertips, then slipped it over so they could watch the image appear. He tilted the tray back and forth, propelling a steady stream of liquid across the paper.

"It's starting to come," he said, excitement sounding in his voice. "Look."

There formed before them through the liquid a kitchen scene. Birch cupboards with curved handles, microwave, spices neatly ordered on a large spice rack. A wide oval table with salt and pepper mills on it. In the foreground, on the table, a large, gutted salmon lay across sheets of rumpled newspaper.

"It looks unreal, doesn't it? Out of place?"

She answered with another question. "Who caught it?"

"You have to be careful you don't leave it in too long," he said, slipping the print quickly out of the Dektol and into the stop bath. "This stops the developing." He worked the liquid over it as he had with the previous tray. "And now into the fixer for a while," he said, and transferred the print into the last tray.

"That's it?"

"Except for the washing. We wait out the time and switch the lights back on and really get a good look at what we have."

He kept an eye on his digital watch. The seconds squeezed into each other. He tried to ignore it after looking at it three times in the first half minute. The silence had grown shameful.

He turned and looked at Elaine. She smiled softly, uncomfortably. He held back for only a second, then approached her lips, determined to see through a sudden impulse.

They kissed. He could feel a moment of pleasure in her response. Withdrawing, he turned back quickly to the print, to avoid having to see her reaction.

He kept his eyes on his watch. Without saying anything he stood up and opened the door. Light plunged into the room, causing both their faces to cringe for protection.

Nine

The teacher, Langman, dressed in a checked flannel shirt and a pair of tan cords, sat on a corner of the desk, one foot on the floor. Over the past couple of minutes the noise level had risen in anticipation of the bell ringing for the end of the class. Several students were talking, indifferent to his question.

"What image do you think the poet is trying to create?" he asked again.

Lorne could notice his irritation surfacing. "Barnes," he said sharply, "your head on a swivel? Margaret can, you know, get through this class without seeing your face every five seconds."

Barnes turned his head around slowly and looked toward the front, hardly moving the rest of his body. He smiled at Langman, enjoying the attention.

There was momentary quiet. "Can anybody give me an answer?"

"Ask Lorne."

Langman's gaze stopped for a moment on Lorne, who was sitting at the front of one of the side rows, several feet ahead of the next seat. He could see that Lorne was not about to answer again.

"Why write something that takes a half hour to figure out?" Barnes questioned. "And even then you can't prove you're right."

Langman shook his head in amplified frustration. "Obviously to make people suffer! As a form of student torture, what else?"

Some of them laughed. The few who groaned edged him on further.

"You think poetry is something to enjoy?" he said, ranging his voice in mock excitement. "I mean, forget it. It's right up there with needles under the fingernails, head in a vise. It's the killer instinct in poets that makes them want to write. They want you to moan in the agony of picking their poetry apart, looking for meaning that's not there. They want you to suffer your way through exams. Poets are fascinated by the pain they can inflict on innocent, underworked minds."

"Overworked, you mean."

"Innocent?"

"Overworked with some things," Barnes said.

"Okay, Barnes, stop right there before you get us excited. Okay, okay," he said, calming them down, "back to my question."

Barbara now looked willing to attempt an answer. The class had finally quieted down. She began, but the bell broke her sentence after the second word. Laughter erupted again.

Langman snapped his book shut. He stood up and gathered two more from the desk. "There *is* tomorrow," he said as he left, smiling but obviously relieved that the class had ended.

> It does give teachers something to teach
> Probably relevant in years to come
> But school bothers some.
>
> It tells students what to learn
> Force-fed, it tends to numb
> School bothers some.
>
> It takes work to pass
> To graduate. In sum,
> School can be bothersome.

Lorne read it over again. This one was not yet to his satisfaction. Perhaps too superficial, too much like Pink Floyd. He fitted the sheet between the pages of his binder.

While he waited for the next class to begin, he glanced several times across the room at Elaine, being careful not to be obvious about it. He caught her eye and then the trace of a smile. He smiled back and quickly turned his head toward the front.

Ryan, the history teacher, entered the classroom. The noise in the room disappeared as he sat down solidly behind the desk. He opened the text to within a few pages of the section he wanted.

Ryan looked around the room to bring about complete quiet. At the far side of the classroom, near the back, his glance landed on Trevor, head propped up on his hand, leaning against the wall. Trevor's eyes shut and opened quickly a number of times, then shut and remained closed.

"Trevor, are you with us?" Ryan asked.

Trevor's eyes opened; his head swung upright.

"An exhausting night last night?"

"Yes, sir, extremely exhausting." There was a murmur of laughter. "Studying late. Studying history." The laughter increased.

It failed to soften Ryan's expression. "Perhaps then you wouldn't mind telling us the significance of what you read last night."

Trevor glanced down at his book. "The end of the war," he said. "Armistice."

"And what does that mean to you?"

"A day off from school."

There was another short outburst of laughter. Ryan let it continue unchecked. When it died away, he said, "Anything else? What do you think it means to those who fought in the war?"

"For some I guess it means a chance to remember old times. For a lot it's a chance for a good drunk at the Legion."

Ryan came down hard and swift. "Out!" he blasted him, his finger pointing to the door. "Get out!"

It startled the class into silence. Trevor shifted in his seat, sitting more upright, but he made no move to get out of it.

"Did you hear what I told you?"

"I don't think you have the right to kick me out," Trevor said, the words bolder than his voice.

"You don't, do you?"

"I was only giving an opinion."

The class stiffened in anticipation of what Ryan might do next. His arms fell onto the desk, one on each side of the textbook. He pushed back the chair and stood up.

As he walked down the aisle all eyes nervously followed him. He stood behind Trevor's seat, facing the front.

"I'm telling you once more to leave this classroom." He said it slowly, forcing himself to appear calm. "I'm in no mood for any more of your jokes."

Trevor offered no reaction, no compromise.

Ryan grabbed him by the arm and yanked him out of the seat. "When I say get out, I mean it!" He shoved him forward a few steps.

Trevor, although no stronger, stood taller than Ryan. Trevor glared at him, and for an anxious second the look threatened retaliation.

"That's all most of you are here for—a laugh and a good time," Ryan shouted, turning his attention to the faces that surrounded him.

Trevor turned his back on him and walked slowly to the door. "I'm going to see the principal," he said as he opened it.

Within seconds Ryan was out the door and down the corridor behind him.

Ten

As he walked around toward the back door, Lorne saw Trevor's father working under the upraised hood of their pickup. When he turned, Lorne said hello to him.

"This blood-of-a-bitch of a bolt. I'll have the head twist off yet. Here, hand me that WD-40."

Lorne looked through the toolbox that lay on the ground until Trevor's father directed him to the spray can lying next to it. He passed it to him, and he continued to work. When he asked, Lorne told him his name.

"I shoulda known. You looks something like your old man."

"Where will I find Trevor?" Lorne asked.

"Trev is in the house somewhere, or he was a minute ago. Just go on in. The wife'll get him for you."

He walked over to the door and knocked. A voice called from under the hood. "Open the door, my son, and go on in. Go on."

He did so, but inside the porch he found another door. He opened it a fraction with one hand and knocked with the other. A large, curly-headed woman with a dish towel in her hand opened it the rest of the way. She was surprised to see someone she didn't recognize.

"Trevor around?"

She turned down the radio. "He's in the basement, him and Hilary. Down over the steps behind you. Mind now you don't trip over them boots there."

Before he reached the bottom steps he could hear Trevor's laughter cut short by painful groans. The concrete wall opposite him was stacked high with birch firewood. A chopping block stood in front, an ax sunk into the top, a pile of splits to one side.

He traced the sounds past the wood to a room roughly partitioned off from the main part of the basement. Standing in the doorless entrance, he found the two of them wrestling, with Trevor pinned to the floor under his brother.

Hilary tightened and twisted the headlock he had on him. Trevor winced in agony. "You fat-gutted fucker," he groaned.

Trying to ignore the pain, Trevor renewed the effort to free himself with a quick surge of energy. His body rose inches off the carpet, muscle strained stiff against muscle. It lasted only seconds, until Hilary broke the tension and Trevor collapsed back flat to the floor. His body fell limp.

Hilary retreated to an old battered couch. A square of worn-out carpet covered part of the floor, pieces of weight-lifting equipment crowding one corner of it.

On a wall hung a dart board centered on a piece of plywood, both pitted with thousands of tiny holes.

Trevor looked up. His naked upper body was creased red and glistened with sweat. He was rubbing the back of his neck with his hand.

"Lorne," he said. He was quick to cover his surprise. "Whaddaya up to?" He rose to his feet, still rubbing his neck. "That frigger there just about got me killed."

"What's the matter, puss, can't handle it?" Hilary said. Trevor gave him the finger.

Lorne sat down in an old kitchen chair near the door. Trevor sat on the arm of the couch, at the opposite end from his brother, his stocking feet sunk between the cushions.

"Back home for a while?" Lorne said to Hilary.

"Long enough to get myself hung. We're going back to Edmonton in two weeks."

"My son," Trevor said, "Shirley must be nuts to get married to you. She haven't got a clue what she's gettin herself into."

"I knows what *I'll* be gettin *myself* into," Hilary replied, twisting his head and winking.

"By the looks of things you got into it once too often already."

Trevor laughed, relishing the fact that Hilary was stuck for something to say.

When the laughter had died away, Trevor looked at Lorne. Lorne could see he was expecting a reason for his showing up.

"You didn't come to the meeting we had after school," Lorne said.

"Ryan got me kicked out for three days."

"You serious?" Lorne said.

"The prick never did have much use for me."

"And what did Keats say?"

"Fuck all."

"You knows damn well Keats is not going to go against anything Ryan says," Hilary put in. "It was the same thing when I was in school."

Lorne wasn't sure how to react. His mouth moved about uneasily. "Keats is usually pretty decent."

"I dunno," Trevor said. "Ryan had it in his head to get me kicked out. There wasn't anyone going to stop him."

"I'd say if it was me I'da flattened in that fat face of his," Hilary said.

"That's easy enough for you to say. You haven't got to try to pass this year. Ryan is not going to change his mind, I knows that for a fact. And if I goes to Keats again, I'll probably only get in more shit. My history mark is bad enough as it is. I only got one spare subject, and for sure I'll never get through French."

Lorne shook his head. "Fuck!" he said with unexpected intensity. "That's not right."

The other two remained quiet, wondering if there was more. But Lorne could offer no solution.

A voice called down the steps. "Supper is ready."

"Good," Hilary said, jumping up, " 'cause I'm fuckin starved."

"He's such a lousy teacher anyway," Lorne was saying. "If he didn't have a textbook, he wouldn't know what to do."

"Come on up and have some supper," Hilary said to Lorne.

"Thanks. I better be getting home."

"No, you're not," Trevor insisted, jabbing him with his fist.

At the top of the stairs Trevor opened the door to the kitchen. "Set out another place."

Lorne remained in the porch with his hand on the knob of the outside door, ready to leave. Trevor's mother looked out. "You're welcome to stay and have some, you know."

He quietly declined the offer again.

"Go on," Trevor's father said, "don't talk so foolish. Trev, take hes coat, look, and go get another chair."

Lorne sat wedged between Trevor and one of his two sisters. He counted seven people in all crowded around the small kitchen table.

Trevor's father forked a steaming potato onto Lorne's plate. "Now," he said, passing him the platter of fish, "take hold. Don't go away from the table hungry."

Eleven

Ryan took no notice of the complete quiet of the classroom when he entered. Perhaps he thought the stapled test papers he brought with him were explanation enough for their behavior.

He gave his standard caution. "I don't want to hear any talking when you're finished; just turn over your papers and stay quiet."

He deposited a copy of the test facedown before each of the students. "For once I don't have to tell you to clear the books off the top of your desks," he said. When he had finished, every desk, with one exception, bore a paper. He sat down at his own desk, positioned the leftover papers neatly to one side and opened a copy of *Maclean's* magazine in front of him.

"You may begin," he said, without looking up.

No one in the classroom moved to turn over a paper.

"Go ahead, you can start," he said, looking directly at them this time.

Still no one reacted. A few stared back at him. Some eased their discomfort by gazing at the back of the person in front of them. Others nervously rolled their pens across the papers.

"All right, what's going on?"

Nobody would answer. The fact that they all remained so solemn heightened his irritation. It was clear they weren't doing it in fun. He surveyed their faces, looking for signs of weakness. He caught Barnes glancing across the aisle, mouthing words to Lorne.

He jumped at that. "Barnes, just what's this all about?" he said forcefully.

Barnes quickly turned his head. He hesitated to the point that Ryan was set to blast him further.

A voice intruded. "We're on strike," it said.

The color in Ryan's face deepened. But discovering that it was Lorne who had spoken, he suppressed the outburst that had seemed inevitable.

"We're protesting Trevor's suspension," Lorne said in a strong, controlled voice. "We believe it was unfair and that he should be allowed back."

Ryan was stunned. His silence caused mumbles of agreement to surface in several parts of the classroom.

"All right, that's enough," he said to no one person in particular. "Your behavior is foolish and immature. And pointless. You've been watching too much television."

"We're protesting for good reason," Lorne said.

Ryan looked at him. "Trevor was suspended with

just cause. I have no intention of reversing that decision. Lorne, if you and the rest of the class don't give this up, you will be in serious danger of being given zeros on this test."

Some of the students, including Elaine, shifted about in their seats, exchanging anxious looks. Lorne waited, but nobody said anything. Eventually he spoke again. "Mr. Ryan, if we didn't believe you were wrong, we wouldn't be doing it."

Ryan looked hard at Lorne. When Lorne only stared back, Ryan's eyes turned to his desk. He shuffled his papers into the pages of his magazine.

The class waited. "Okay," Ryan said with renewed anger, "if that's the way you want it, we'll just have to see what Mr. Keats has to say about this." His chair scraped backward to give him room to stand up.

"I gave you a chance." He walked away from them, out the door, and down the hallway.

Twelve

The fourth place setting was for his grandmother. It balanced his mother's arrangement of china and silverware on the finely crocheted tablecloth. Crystal wine and water glasses stood at each setting. In the center of the table, on a crystal stand of the same pinwheel pattern as the glasses, was a cake, its white icing edged with pink rosebuds and ringed on top by a double row of small unlit candles. "Happy 62nd Birthday," the lettering read.

In the adjoining living room Lorne sat looking through back issues of *National Geographic*. His mother, an apron protecting her new dress, stood in front of the bow window.

"All this rain makes me uneasy," she said.

"He'll be okay," Lorne said. "He's driven that road enough times."

His grandmother had put her knitting to rest in her lap. "He'll take hes time," she reassured her.

Lorne's mother sat down in the rocker near the window but did not rock. She stared at Lorne, who continued to hold his eyes to the magazine.

His grandmother ended a row of stitches and stopped again. "I never heard Alice complain about Mr. Ryan when she was going to school, and she done fine."

"Gran, I'm not Alice, okay?" he said after a time, without raising his eyes from the pages. He added quietly, "Alice never complained about anything in her life."

"No more she didn't," his grandmother answered, "and she was no worse off for it either."

"You don't understand."

"The man's only got to the end of the year, Lorne, and he's retired," his mother said.

Lorne looked up. He chose his mother to give his attention to. "He had no right to do what he did. Somebody's got to draw the line somewhere. Whadda you think we should do—ignore it, like it never happened? Students have rights, too, you know."

"I could understand it if it was anything important. From what I've heard, Trevor haven't got much of a chance of passing history anyway. He's hardly done any work all year."

"Bullshit!"

"Lorne!" his grandmother said in disgust. "What's got wrong with you?"

He would have got up from the chair and left the

room, but he heard his father's car come into the driveway.

"He's here, thank goodness," his mother said. "Now we can eat."

They listened as Lorne's father removed his overshoes and hung his raglan in the closet.

"How's the birthday girl?" he called out.

He came into the living room carrying a foil-wrapped pot overflowing with the blossoms of a red azalea. He presented it to his mother.

"Dear, it's beautiful."

Before they sat down to eat, Lorne's mother set the plant on the dining-room buffet opposite her mother-in-law's place at the table. A platter of baked ham together with several covered dishes of vegetables were brought from the kitchen and put on the table. His father unscrewed the top from the bottle of wine.

The table was covered with food. Lorne took a piece of the sliced ham, some raisin sauce, and small portions of three of the vegetables.

"He hardly eats enough to keep a jay alive."

Lorne paid no notice. He ate without comment except when someone spoke directly to him. The others talked about the weather, what movie was coming on TV, and how well Alice was doing at university.

When the plates were taken away, Lorne's mother moved the cake in front of his grandmother. His father lit the candles. On the slow count of three the old woman blew at the ring of tiny flames. It took a second, equally forceful breath to extinguish them all. Lorne had flashed the picture before her pause and captured the full impact of her first effort. Anybody looking at the picture would think that she was certain to get her wish.

She cut large pieces of cake for him and his father and pieces half that size for his mother and herself.

When Lorne had eaten most of his, he set the plate aside and moved his chair away from the table. "Excuse me, I have an assignment to work on."

"Lorne, I talked to Mr. Ryan today on the phone." His father put his fork on the edge of the plate. "He says this is bound to affect your final mark."

The timing of his father's words caught Lorne by surprise. He stood up, pushing the chair in tight against the table.

"I'm not sure you know what you're doing," his father added.

"*I* am," Lorne said.

They waited, but he said nothing more. "Are you taking time to figure out the possible consequences of all this?"

"Dad, I know what I'm doing."

"You might think you do. Is it that important that you can sacrifice your marks?"

"To me it is."

"I don't understand you, Lorne. Trevor's suspension would have been forgot about in a couple of days."

He stood there, staring at his father, frustrated at knowing the uselessness of trying to argue with him.

His mother's words followed him as he left the room. "You could make yourself look foolish in the end," she said.

There was no answer.

"Independent," he could hear her say. "I never saw the like, the way he's been here lately."

"Too independent for his own good," the old woman added.

Thirteen

Lorne watched as Ryan's car turned from the main road onto the school access. He slowed down immediately as if he needed time to decide whether he could be the reason for this mass of students, many with placards, marching outside the school. Their attention turned quickly to his car and all doubt must have faded.

He obviously had no intention of parking anyplace other than where he always parked. He blew the horn to speed newly arrived students out of his way. Turning off the ignition, he leaned across and locked the passenger door. Once outside, he tried his own door to check that it was also locked.

He walked in front of the other cars toward the main entrance to avoid direct contact with any of the students. But he didn't escape several taunting shouts from the crowd.

"Suspend Ryan!" someone yelled. Others tried to turn it into a chant. Ryan ignored it.

"Don't retire him, fire him!" came another yell. Lorne told the guy to shut up.

Ryan could see who it was. He walked angrily toward the students. Without speaking he shoved aside the person in front and make a grab for Barnes. He fastened both his hands on his jacket and drew them tight.

"What did you say?"

Barnes instantly locked his own hands around Ryan's wrists. With a forceful downward jerk he dislodged them. One hand tightened into a fist. He held it threateningly at chest level in front of Ryan.

Lorne forced himself between them.

"Calm down!" he told Barnes.

"Man, I'm not going to hit him. He's too old to hit."

Lorne turned to Ryan, blocking his view of Barnes. "Mr. Ryan, take it easy. Nobody wants anybody getting hurt."

"Do you realize what you have here, Lorne? A bunch of loudmouths throwing insults, whose only reason for being out here in the first place is to get a day off from school!"

A wave of booing started in the back of the crowd. Ryan turned around and walked toward the school. The booing intensified as the distance between Ryan and the students increased. When he opened the door and stepped inside, the noise climaxed, surrounding Lorne, leaving him motionless.

Near noon Lorne and Trevor entered the school for

a meeting with the principal and Ryan. They walked into the principal's office and sat down in chairs brought in for them by the secretary.

"No need for preliminaries," Keats said. "I'll come right to the point. I've been on the phone to the superintendent. The school board feels your protest is unnecessary and unwarranted, and they're making a strong suggestion that all students return to classes this afternoon."

Trevor looked surprised by the abruptness of the statement. He unfolded his arms and looked at Lorne. Lorne did not alter his stare, even as his jaw began to shift about nervously.

"On condition that Trevor be allowed back in class and that he receives an apology from Mr. Ryan," Lorne said firmly.

Lorne had sounded equally abrupt. They turned their attention to Trevor.

"Your suspension stands as it is," Keats said.

Trevor tried to work up a response. It gave Ryan an opening.

"I won't be changing my mind. It's about time you people learned to put up with the consequences if you're going to dish out insults."

The principal intervened. "A solution is not simple," he said, trying to prevent a further widening of the gap between them. "The thing is, we don't want students losing any more valuable school time. Do we?" He waited for Lorne to answer.

Lorne looked at him intently. "We could go to the media," he said.

The principal drew back. "I don't think that would do anybody any good," Keats told him.

"We're considering it." He held up his camera enclosed in its leather case. "Pictures for publication in the newspaper."

Lorne looked at Ryan.

Ryan hesitated. Trevor jumped in as if he had smelled revenge. "Probably give CBC a call and see if they would send out a TV crew," he said.

They waited on Ryan. The man's face grew stiff with anger.

"That's not going to prove much," the principal said, dismissing Trevor's remark as if he had been naive to make it.

But Lorne could sense the uncertainty. "Perhaps," he said, "we should start serious discussions about why we're protesting in the first place."

The principal leaned forward. "We were willing to do that all along."

Depending on what was said next, Lorne decided, he would let that pass.

"I suggest this," Keats said in earnest. "You get the students back in class, and we'll allow Trevor back for the time being. On probation."

Looking at Trevor, Lorne tried to gauge his feelings.

"Sounds reasonable," Trevor told them before Lorne had time to say anything.

Fourteen

Lorne stood next to him as Trevor worked at the combination to his locker. In the noise of students crowding out the exit at the end of the day, their conversation was as private as if it had been only the two of them.

"Ah, the hell with it," Trevor said. "I can live with that. If he does write one, he won't mean it."

Lorne was not satisfied. "That's letting him off too easy."

"It's not worth the trouble. Besides, we won't get the support from all the students like we did before. There's a lot that wouldn't walk out again over that. I say let's leave it. It's no big deal."

Lorne couldn't cover his disappointment, yet he saw no point in arguing. "All right," he said.

"Sure?"

"Yeah."

"No, you're not. I mean, you put your ass on the line for me."

"Maybe you're right. Maybe it wouldn't prove anything," he said. "You're going to miss the bus."

Trevor moved away. "Drop over to the house later on," he said, looking back.

Lorne walked farther along the corridor to his own locker and opened it. He stared at the books, trying to decide which ones to take out. Finally he closed the door on them all, attached the lock, and rammed it shut.

He continued along the corridor to the classroom at the end. He could see Ryan at the desk inside, correcting papers, the only person there. Ryan looked up long enough to see who it was, and then he turned back to the work in front of him.

"Looking for your mark?" he said.

"No," Lorne answered, walking toward the desk.

Ryan counted up the marks scattered over several pages of the exam and wrote the total on the top right-hand corner of the front page. He recorded it in a thick spiral book near him.

He looked at Lorne, who was now standing within a few feet of the desk. "What is it you want?" he said bluntly.

"We've decided to accept the situation as it stands. There'll be no more walkouts."

Ryan began correcting another exam. "Good," he said.

Lorne stayed where he was until the continuing silence turned him away. He was almost out the door.

"But you're not satisfied, is that it?"

He stopped and looked back. "It was not my decision."

Ryan put down his pen. "You know, in all the time I've been teaching this is the first time anything like this has ever happened. I just thought you should know that. The first year I taught all I had was my high school diploma and two months of summer school. I had sole charge of a one-room school—thirty-eight students, seven different grades. Some of the students were older than I was. You had to be strict, but there was such a thing as respect for teachers. I was the same age as you are now. You think you could have handled that?"

Lorne decided it better not to answer. He saw no point in adding more fuel for argument.

"The next year I signed up in the Newfoundland Regiment and went overseas."

Again he waited, inviting a response. None came.

"I had a call from your father last night."

A further prod? Lorne turned again to leave.

"Lorne."

He looked back.

"Some things you don't learn by being told," Ryan said to him.

"Perhaps, Mr. Ryan, there are some things you shouldn't be trying to teach."

He left the room.

Out in the corridor Lorne almost ran into Elaine, who was just coming out of the music room with her guitar case in her hand.

"I could do with a new pair of glasses," he said.

He could see that she sensed his uneasiness.

"You think I did the right thing?"

She looked at him, puzzled.

"The strike?" he prompted.

"You did what you felt you had to."

"But you didn't agree with it."

"I didn't say that." There was a slight note of anger in her voice. "My mother was a teacher, remember."

"I didn't mean . . ." He looked away. "I got to go," he said. "I'm sorry." He left her standing alone in the middle of the corridor.

"I'll phone you," she called out to him as he walked quickly out the front entrance.

Fifteen

Langman handed Lorne another print.

"Candid, eh? Candid photography? Whoa, eh? Whoa, eh?"

Without fail, any long conversation he had with Langman touched off at some point a reference to one of the insane sketches from Monty Python. "Their new movie is out on videotape. You'll have to come over and watch it when I get it in," Langman said.

"I still got your album. I'll try to remember to bring it to school on Monday."

Langman passed him another print, one of several of his young daughter. "I like that one," Lorne said. "I like the angle you shot it from."

"The angle makes all the difference. Sometimes you see things you wouldn't really think are there."

After Lorne viewed each one, he passed it along to

Elaine, who was seated next to him on the couch. Langman placed a partial bottle of white wine on the coffee table, together with some glasses. He lowered the volume of the McCartney music playing on the stereo and sat down. Leaning over, he filled a glass for himself and one for Lorne. Elaine said she didn't really want any.

"Did you work on that poem again?" he asked Lorne.

"A bit."

"Satisfied with it?"

"Not really."

"I didn't know you wrote poetry," Elaine said, turning her attention from the pictures.

"Sorry," Langman said. "I didn't mean to give away any secrets."

"It's not something I talk about much," Lorne told Elaine.

"I'd like to read some."

"They're not very good."

"The ones you showed me are," Langman said. "He's just being modest."

Lorne's silent embarrassment ended the discussion.

Elaine turned back to the pictures. When she finished with them, she placed them carefully on the corner of the coffee table.

"Michelle wants to make sure Sarah is asleep before we go. She shouldn't be any trouble. If she does wake up, she might want a drink of juice or something."

They sat back and sipped the wine.

"Are you satisfied with the way things worked out at school?" Langman asked him.

"Ryan still won't admit he was wrong. He still refuses to apologize to Trevor."

Langman sat forward in the chair, his hands cupping the wineglass between his knees. "Perhaps," he said, "that's too much to expect."

Lorne was dismayed. "You went to high school in the sixties," he argued. "You took part in demonstrations when you were in university, you told me that."

He smiled. "When I was in grade nine, I was kicked out of school for two weeks because I refused to get my hair cut."

"Serious?"

"Long hair was a big deal in those days."

"Then I can't see why you don't agree with me."

"It's not that."

Lorne looked at him for an explanation.

"I guess I have to look at it from his point of view too. He's due to retire in a few weeks. . . ."

"I can't see that. I really can't. Where do you draw the line? When do you stop compromising for the sake of someone's feelings?"

"I can't answer that one. Perhaps you're making too much of what happened. Maybe you're looking too hard for something to fight against. . . ."

Langman shrugged.

Finally Elaine stepped in. "There's no point in arguing over it. I can understand the way you both feel."

Later, when Langman and his wife had gone and Lorne was alone with Elaine except for Sarah in bed, he felt he had to bring it up again.

"I just feel sorry for Mr. Ryan sometimes," Elaine said. "He lives alone, he was never married, he has no family here."

"I think that's irrelevant to the situation," he said.
"But you can't look at it in isolation."

"You have to," he said as gently as he could, hoping
she would sense that he didn't really want to pursue
the matter and risk an argument.

He turned on the TV set. During the opening com-
mercials they drew closer on the couch. By the time
the movie started his arm was around her shoulders.
His other hand rested comfortably in hers.

It was a second-rate horror movie. Given the cir-
cumstances in which he found himself, he watched it
with interest.

> Held in fright, she twisted
> my hand, our hearts that night
> At the sight of bloodied knives
> she sank her face in my chest
> My heartbeat leapt.
> I promised peace
> A nervous arm gave support
> for a momentary touch of breast
> I loved her near
> her exaggerated, unconvincing fear
> for me to lay to rest.
> I wanted more—
> to lovingly restore
> a more pleasurable calm
> A lengthened kiss relaxed
> her fears, inviting me
> to wander tenderly
> along the softness of her limbs.
> To stop at this or to go on.
> My dread at offending her instead

      intensified, so at movie's end
      I lay tightly clothed
      At rest, at arousing rest.

A car turned into the driveway. They both sat up quickly. Lorne moved to the armchair as Elaine sat brushing her hair loose with her fingers. When Langman and his wife came in, they apologized for being longer than they had expected. Lorne said not to worry, there had been some good programs on television. Elaine tried not to smile.

Sixteen

While he waited he lay back on his bed in a square of evening sun and leafed through a photography magazine. He stopped a couple of times at pictures by Cartier-Bresson to consider the possibility of cutting them out later and tacking them up with the others on his bedroom walls.

His thoughts wandered to Elaine. He was happy with the way things were moving along. He was actually getting somewhere with a girl. It felt good, a relief to know that someone he liked wanted to go out with him. Her shyness was a help. He liked the way they were both losing it around each other. He turned over onto his stomach, imagining what it could lead to.

About eight o'clock a car with a faulty muffler turned onto the shoulder of the road in front of the house. He got up and tossed the magazine back onto his desk. He could hear the driver revving the motor instead of blowing the horn. Going into the kitchen, he saw that the noise had sent his mother to the window.

On his way to the back door he passed by his father, who had just begun supper at the kitchen table.

"I'm going into St. John's tomorrow," his father said. "Anything you want? Another cartridge for the Atari?"

"I haven't used that in months," Lorne told him.

His mother followed him out of the kitchen. "Where you going?" she asked as he tied his sneakers.

"Out."

"You be careful, Lorne. That car doesn't sound very safe to me."

He stood up straight and gathered his jacket from the closet while his mother continued to talk.

"Now, don't be too late," she said.

"If I don't show up, I'm spending the night over at Trevor's place." He went out the door, leaving it to close on its own.

Trevor stretched across the front seat and forced the passenger door open.

"The lock is screwed up," he told him after Lorne had slid into the seat. "How's it goin?"

"Not bad," he said, hauling on the door but failing to close it.

"Give er shit," Trevor told him.

He pushed it open wide and pulled on it as hard as he could. This time it shut. Trevor turned the car back noisily onto the road.

"Muffler trouble?" Lorne said, grinning.

"The pipe is broke just past the resonator. I'm after having the lousy thing welded once."

"Too bad."

"That's fuck all. As long as she gets me where I'm going."

Lorne sat there wishing he had something to do, like light up a cigarette.

"Where we goin?" Lorne asked.

"I dunno. We'll see who's on the go. The stag is not startin till about nine."

"Hilary lookin forward to it?"

"He says he is. I don't know what the hell for, though. I figure he'll be pukin hesself silly before the night is over."

Trevor was laughing. Lorne felt more relaxed.

"We'll take it easy," Trevor said, "fuck around for a while. We could use a good tear after the week we've had. Can't let things get too serious, or there's no point to it."

Lorne thought perhaps he could agree with that. Right now he would, at least.

They cruised along the stretch of road between Marten and Spencer's. They topped Pinsent's Grade doing 120 kilometers an hour.

"When you gettin your license?" Trevor asked him.

"Hard to say," Lorne answered hesitantly. "Probably the summer."

"I figured you'da had em by now. That car your old man got should be able to haul ass."

"She's not bad."

"What's in her, a three-eighteen?"

Lorne took his time in answering; too much time, he

knew. "Something like that," he said, trying to sound offhanded about it.

"Jesus, the cops!" Trevor bellowed. His right foot jumped to the brake. A police car had rounded a curve about half a kilometer up the road. "If that's Olson, we're fucked."

He eased the car down to the speed limit. Then, with the police car just ahead, he turned the key to cut the engine and the roar of the exhaust. They drifted past the police car noiselessly. He checked the rearview mirror, turning his head as little as possible. Nothing flashing. The cops had kept on going.

"Close." He sighed, more than pleased with himself. Once the police were no longer visible in the mirror, he turned the key back. The car bucked slightly. He floored her. The exhaust roared.

A short distance ahead they saw the entrance sign to Spencer's. Trevor cut back the speed again. As he drove along they saw a group of girls sitting on the steps of the community hall. He blew the horn at them.

Gwen was one of them. She held up her hand. Trevor groaned.

"Jesus," he said, "I got a good mind to slip the dick into that one of these nights. There'd be no sweat to do it either."

"She's not bad," Lorne said.

"You wouldn't kick her outta the sack."

They drove to the end of Spencer's, past the bus turnaround, and down a side road. There they found a car parked, with four people inside. Trevor turned in alongside it, so that the drivers' sides faced each other. He rolled down the window.

"What's happenin, b'ys?"

"This is it."

"Any stuff on the go?"

"Nothin. This place is as dry as a fuckin bone."

"The boys got none o' that black left?"

"Sold the last gram last night."

"What, Hilary's oil all gone?"

"Fuck, that was gone three days after he got home, old man. Wicked stuff while it lasted," Trevor said.

"Hey, Lorne, want a brew?" one of them shouted from the backseat. "Boys, give the strike leader a fuckin beer."

"What about me?" Trevor complained.

"You, you're fuck all, you're only the jerk that caused it," someone said, laughing.

They handed across two beers. "Careful, the cops is down."

"We know." Trevor proceeded to recount the details of his near miss a few minutes before. Lorne had turned sideways in the seat, his arm resting on the dash. The warm beer slipped down easily.

A half hour later they headed for the stag party. By eleven o'clock Lorne had drunk more beer than he ever had before.

Someone snapped the cap off another bottle and slid it along the table in his direction before he had the one in his hand half gone. He had managed to steer clear of the whiskey and rum bottles that littered the tables. Trevor's warning about mixing his drinks had somehow stuck with him.

"You okay?" Trevor asked.

"Perfect." He grinned at him. "Fuck it."

Someone showed up with a VHS machine. The TV

screen lit up with the start of the tape. "Someone shuff off the lights."

He saw all he could of it through his drunken vision. It was definitely straight to the point. The actors were out of their clothes within the first five minutes.

"That's what I call beating around the bush," Trevor called out. It was the start of a round of comments that kept the place roaring with laughter.

Lorne had not seen anything like it before. The magazines were nothing compared to this. He felt as if he had just joined in on a great secret.

At the first dull spot in the movie he was ready for another beer.

"See how fast you can chug it down."

"Forget it," Lorne said.

"C'mon, I'll time ya," Trevor urged him.

"No friggin way," he muttered.

"C'mon."

He raised the bottle to his mouth and started to drink. The beer slid down his throat, swallow after swallow.

"Keep goin, keep goin!"

He kept it there, forcing down more and more, till he almost reached the last of it. The bottle fell from his lips. His guts urged, his mouth parted, and a wild gush of beer spewed forth uncontrollably, spraying like a wave splattered against a rock. Across the table Trevor snapped his head away, but it was too late. The beer that a second before had been in Lorne's stomach dripped from Trevor's face and hair.

The table exploded in laughter. It pulled the attention of everybody else in the room to Lorne.

Seventeen

All five of them headed toward the wharf and the fish plant. Two couples and Gwen. She lingered between them, a part of neither.

It was the warmest day yet in May, warm enough for Lorne to carry his sweater instead of wearing it. Trevor had left his jacket back at the house. He slipped his cigarette pack between his T-shirt and the bulge of muscle in his upper arm. He smoked as he walked, Barbara telling him again that he should be giving it up.

"You got to die sometime. If the butt don't do the job on ya, something else will."

"Your logic amazes me," she said.

Lorne held Elaine's hand. He was pleasantly surprised that it felt so comfortable in public.

Gwen followed behind the two couples. Her sudden

silence cautioned them against ignoring her for very much longer.

Elaine could sense her irritation. "Gwen," she asked, "have you heard Mr. Ryan say anything about the project since the strike?"

"Nothing."

"I wonder if he's changed his mind?"

"About what?"

"Letting us do an interview with him."

"Forget it," Trevor said. "No friggin way."

"Maybe you're not, but I am," Barbara said. "I want a good mark on this. And he knows more about the history of this place than anybody else."

"Forget it," Trevor said again.

Lorne looked at Barbara. "Isn't there anybody else we can go to?"

"Like who?" she said point-blank.

"I don't know."

"How about your grandmother?" Gwen said to Lorne.

"Who, *my* grandmother?"

"She's supposed to have a really good memory. I've heard Mom say that," Elaine said.

Lorne hesitated. "Maybe. That's one possibility."

"Ask her and see what she says?" Elaine added quickly.

"We'll see."

"We haven't got that much time," Barbara told him. "The deadline is the twenty-fifth."

"She's right. It's time we did something."

"Right," Trevor said, "cut the bullshitting around and get to work."

"That's a switch," Barbara said.

"Ryan is dyin to give us a crappy mark on this, I bet you the frig he is. We gotta show him something that he got no choice but give us an *A* for," Trevor said.

There could be no argument with that. They looked for Lorne's reaction.

He raised the camera high over his head.

"Go for it!" Trevor proclaimed.

"And give er shit!" Lorne reaffirmed.

Over the next hour he went through a full roll of film. They had arrived at the wharf at a perfect time. There were two long-liners unloading codfish, one of them owned by Trevor's father. The cod, hundreds of pounds of it at a time, was being loaded into a bulky orange net in the boat's hold. Hoisted then up and over the wharf, its weight recorded, the net was let open to release the fish into large gray tubs for transfer into the fish plant.

As Lorne snapped pictures Trevor jumped aboard the boat and talked to his father. After a while his father shouted for the others to come aboard as well.

"This the first time you've been aboard a long-liner?"

Lorne admitted that it was.

"The summer, when you get out of school, you'll have to come out with us for a day. The capelin'll be on the go then."

He said, "I'd like that."

Back at Barbara's, in the rec room in the basement, they tried to get their ideas in order. Except for Trevor they were all sitting around the card table Barbara had set up in the center of the room.

"The slides and the interviews should make up a big part of it, but what about the narration?"

"We got to present it some way so that it's not boring."

"I know," Trevor called out from the bar on the other side of the room, where he was looking through the cabinets. "The girls can parade across the stage in string bikinis . . . that should keep them interested."

"Very funny." Barbara sneered. "And you better get outta there. Dad'll have your head."

"All the good stuff's locked up anyway," he said. He joined the others at the table.

"I'm not sure how we can do it," Barbara said.

"We should try to keep it brief and to the point," Elaine suggested. "Let the pictures do the talking, narrate it in poetry or something."

"You're kidding, poetry?" Gwen said. "This is getting weirder all the time."

"Weird, very weird."

"I can see Ryan's face now."

Even Barbara was apprehensive. "None of us can write poetry."

Elaine didn't defend her suggestion, and neither did she look at Lorne, but it was clear enough to him that she expected him to say something.

"It's different," Lorne said. "Why not?"

"Are you serious? Come off it."

"I've written a bit of poetry. I'm willing to give it a try."

"The guy is a blood-of-a-bitch for punishment," Trevor said.

"We don't have to stick with it," Lorne was quick to add, "just see if it works. If not, we do it another way."

Nobody gave a definite no.

"After all," Lorne said, "that's how great discoveries are made, right, when someone's got the guts to try something different."

Eighteen

He approached the back steps with the consolation that it should take only a few minutes. The house needed painting. Something else not to look forward to. Matched sets of curtains hung on the clothesline, and several mats hung over the railing. She was cleaning for spring.

The house inside seemed even cleaner than it had been when his grandfather was alive. He walked through to the kitchen. His grandmother looked across the room, surprised.

"A stranger," she said.

"I just dropped by for a few minutes."

As soon as the words were out he regretted saying what he had, realizing he was already sounding impatient. He slipped off his sneakers and walked across the tiled floor to the rocking chair. He immediately began to rock. Heat streamed out from the wood stove nearby.

"You got it plenty warm here."

"Take off your jacket," she said, sitting down at the kitchen table.

He did so. He folded it and laid it in his lap.

"How's school?" she asked.

"Okay," he said, and waited for her to take it further.

She didn't, so he continued. "That's really why I came to see you. Well, part of it."

She moved aside the empty teacup that was on the table in front of her and brushed the crumbs near it to the edge and into her hand. She put them in the saucer.

"I need some help for a history project. There's a group of us, five. We need to find out more about the history of Marten and the places around. Would it be okay if we came in with a tape recorder and asked you a few questions?"

"Maybe there's not a big lot I can tell you," she said.

"I've heard you tell all kinds of stories."

"Perhaps you might be better off taking your tape recorder somewhere else. There's people who could give you a lot more information than I could. One person in particular."

He didn't have to ask who she was referring to. There was no point in saying anything more. Now he wanted to leave.

The quiet was maddening. He knew he shouldn't have come.

"Stay there, I'll show you something." She left the kitchen. He could hear her climb the stairs.

He had no idea what to expect. He considered leaving but concluded it would only make it harder the next time. In a minute she was back in the kitchen. She placed a small cardboard box on the table and sat down in the chair again. She removed the cover.

"Come over and sit here."

It was a box of old photographs. "I should get these put into an album." She searched through till she found the one she was looking for. "Here it is. This is what Marten looked like when I was a young girl."

Lorne took the photograph from her hand. It was small and yellowed, with scalloped edges. He held it closer to study the details. The landforms were the same. It had to be taken from exactly the same spot where he had been on the top of the Head.

"Did you take the picture?"

"Your grandfather did, just before we were married. It was a hard climb up, but it was such a beautiful view. I haven't been up there since."

The road below was narrower, unpaved; the houses more scattered. Wooden fish flakes for drying cod covered much of the land near the shoreline. Tall masted schooners filled the cove.

"The Labrador Fishery was in full swing then. You'd see as many as a dozen schooners in this cove the one time. You'd hardly credit it could be so beautiful."

"Imagine," he said, "if he could have used a thirty-five millimeter."

"We knew what work is, I can tell you. In the summer there'd hardly be a man in the cove, and it'd be the women who'd have to tend the gardens, raise the sheep and the pigs, besides keepin house and lookin out to the youngsters. And when the schooners come back in the fall, then there'd be all that fish to dry."

She showed him another from the box. The church as it once had looked, with her and his grandfather and their children standing in front. She named each of them.

"Who is this?" he asked, taking up a picture of a young man.

"Your father," she said. "He was eighteen when that was taken."

Lorne could hardly believe it. The person was slender, almost handsome, in spite of the clothes that looked too big for him. His hair was short and neatly combed away from his forehead. He smiled with quiet pride next to a black car that gleamed, highly polished, in the sunlight.

He finally put the picture back between some others in the box. He looked at a few more—couples sitting on the grass beside picket fences, kids dirty-faced with chocolate custard, a funeral procession.

He lifted out one of a group of young people lined against a white clapboard building. The building had to be a school. He studied individual faces to see if there were any whose features he recognized. He showed the picture to his grandmother and asked who they were.

"That's just an old picture taken when I was going to school," she said, drawing it from his hand.

"Which one are you?"

She pointed to a person in the back row. He leaned

over but was only able to get a glimpse of it before she returned it to the box.

"I never did take a very good picture," she said as she slowly put the cover back in place.

Nineteen

And out the bay
in calmer times off Halfway Rock
we threw the jiggers overboard
They sank to what he said
was their accustomed place
We hauled the lines and let free
hauled and let free
until one was struck
by something fierce
Hand over hand
over line-chafed hand I pulled
It broke the surface
and splashed its twenty pounds
I heaved it aboard
the awesome cod, the fearsome brute
to squirm among the four of us.

Elaine jumped clear of the fish flopping in the inch of dirty water that had collected in the bottom of the boat. Bent down over it, Trevor worked the jigger out from its gills. It continued to squirm about.

"The biggest one yet," Lorne said, adjusting his camera.

They jigged for a half hour after that, each of them taking turns. Two more cod were hauled aboard, but neither was as big as the one Lorne had caught.

They wound in the lines, and Trevor started up the outboard again. They clipped along to a point farther out the bay, slowing down only long enough for Trevor to take a leak over the stern.

Just off Squid Island they sighted an iceberg. It floated tall and broad, blue-white with a rounded peak that jutted high at one end, sloping like a ski jump all the way to the opposite end. They circled it twice until Lorne decided on the angle he needed. He wanted to get closer, but Trevor cautioned that sometimes icebergs can flip over without warning.

A second boat approached. It was much bigger than their own, and carried close to a dozen people, each wearing a bright orange life jacket. Trevor explained who it must be long before the boat was close enough for anyone to be recognized—the fellow from the mainland who had set up a business conducting tours of the bay for tourists.

As the boat neared them and the iceberg, they could see him in the bow of the boat, a sou'wester on his head, talking, explaining things between bouts of playing a jig on a button accordion.

"Looks retarded if you ask me," Trevor said. "I wonder how much he ripped them off?"

The boat slowed and began to circle the iceberg. Cameras clicked incessantly. The boat cut near them, and several of the tourists turned their attention and their cameras away from the iceberg and onto the four of them.

Trevor insisted that they all smile. "You want them to think there's such a thing as a real live Newfoundlander who's not friendly?"

Trevor waved, and they waved back at intervals until their boat disappeared around the end of the iceberg. "They loved it," he said.

He leaned the boat away, leaving the iceberg behind, and headed across the bay. He opened her out, giving them plenty of reason to zipper up their jackets and tighten together in pairs for protection from the wind.

When they reached Birchy Cove they searched along the shore until Trevor found what he called Indian Hole—a cavelike channel in through the rock cliff. With the tide up it was wide enough to scull the boat through and along to the patch of pebbly beach at the end of the passage. They jumped from the boat and hauled it up on shore until it held solid.

In the dim light they explored the beach. After several yards it ended in a wall of rock.

"Beothucks used to come in here," Trevor explained.

"What for?"

"Haven't got a clue. To get laid probably. Get a lend of the old man's canoe on a Saturday night and pick up the girlfriend. Then flatten er down here and go right to it."

"Make no wonder you can't pass history."

Trevor took out his wallet and produced a joint. He rounded it into shape and lit it.

"Here," he said, offering it around, "have a whiff." Only Elaine refused, although Trevor ended up smoking most of it.

A few minutes later they had split into couples, a pair on each side of the boat. Lorne stretched out on his side on the rocks, head propped up on his hand, the water lapping up to within a few inches of his feet. He tossed pebbles into the water. Elaine sat near him, looking out toward the light of the opening. When she turned, the light outlined her profile. He stared at her, thinking how attractive she looked.

"It's funny," he said. "The two of us."

She turned her head and looked at him.

"We've been in the same class for years now," he said, "and suddenly we're going out together."

"It's not so funny, really. I've always liked you. You're . . ."

"Shy?"

She smiled. "Serious. Mature, not like some of the others. Like you've got big plans for the future. Do you?"

"Sure, haven't you?"

"I don't know if you'd call them big. I want to go to university."

"I probably will, too, someday. I don't know if I want to right away. I'd like to see a bit of the world, make up my mind about what I really want to do. I guess you know already?"

"Sort of. I think I'd like to work with kids, maybe in a primary school."

"You'd make a great teacher."

"Why do you say that?"

"You got the patience. Little kids like that would drive me nuts."

"I guess I get that from my mother."

Lorne stared at the water for a while, then began playing with the pebbles in front of him.

"Do you believe that," he said, "that you inherit traits from your parents?"

"People always say you do."

"I'm nothing like my parents."

"You must be in some ways."

"None that I can think of."

"You sound like you haven't been getting along with them very well."

"They don't understand me. They can't understand me, we don't think the same way."

Before she could say anything, he sat up next to her and put his arm around her shoulders. "Let's not talk about that," he said.

He kissed her. He kissed her again and drew her down to the rocks, their lips still together.

His mouth wandered to her neck, his hand rubbing slowly back and forth over the curves from her back to her thighs. They could hear smothered laughter from the other side.

He could feel the tightening in his crotch. He pressed it against hers and held it there. He eased the length of her leg up and over his own.

She began pushing against him. She gently forced the two of them apart, kissing him while she did it.

He gave way to her and lay on his back. He smiled to reassure her that he felt no anger. The smile lapsed into embarrassment.

Lorne sat up. Gentle groans, almost lost in the noise
of the water against the shore, drew his glance to the
other side. The light caught the motion of a naked
rear.

Twenty

Trevor had his jacket on, ready to leave Lorne's bed-room.

"You should have no problem with the test," Lorne said.

He wasn't convinced. "It's stupid little mistakes that bring my marks down." He gathered his exercise books from the desk. "Somehow I always manage to fuck up," he said, turning to go out the door.

He came face-to-face with Lorne's mother. Neither he nor Lorne had heard her approach the doorway. His departure came to a sudden halt. Her expression seemed to convince him that smiling his way out of it wouldn't work. She moved aside to let him by.

"Thanks for the lunch. It was really great."

He left without a word from Lorne's mother.

She looked at Lorne. "He's not wasting your time, is he?"

"Whaddaya tryin to say?"

"You can't expect to get good marks if you're not studying yourself."

"We were working together. I was helping him with his French."

"By the noise you were making it didn't sound like you were doing much work. You sure he's not taking advantage, getting you to do work he should be doing himself?"

Lorne walked by her into the hallway. "Can't you just stay out of my affairs for once?"

Moments later she called him back. "Lorne."

She called louder down the hallway a second time. When he finally came into the room she looked at him gravely. "Where did you get what's on your desk?"

"What?"

"You know what."

It struck him suddenly what it was she was talking about. He covered his embarrassment in a snap of anger. "I'd wish people would stop snooping around in my room."

"I wasn't snooping. I came in for the dishes," she said, her voice strained.

He didn't say anything.

"Why do you have that box? Does it belong to Trevor?"

"Mother. . . ."

"I have to know. Now you've given me something else to worry over. It's not enough to come home two o'clock in the morning."

His frustration swelled. He tried to contain it. "Just take the dishes and leave the room, okay?"

"I'm waiting for a sensible answer."

His father came in at that moment. He must have heard them from downstairs.

"What's the matter?" he asked his wife.

Her eyes led him to the desk. He walked over to it and took a closer look. Open on the desk was a small multicolored box with a young, embracing couple on the front. He picked it up and withdrew the contents. He felt one of the three plastic pouches. The ring of pliable rubber inside left no doubt as to what it was. He put them back inside, closed the box, and laid it on the desk.

"You go on out," he said to her. "I'll have a talk with him."

She looked intently at Lorne, without any satisfaction, and then again at her husband. "Perhaps you can get some sense out of him. He won't listen to me." She gathered up the dishes and walked out of the room. "And he might do with a few lessons on how to go about choosing his friends!"

Lorne sat on the side of the bed and leaned back against the headboard. His father, looking equally uncomfortable, closed the door, crowding in the uncertainty. He seated himself in a chair near the desk.

"I don't know what to say to you," he started.

He searched for more words.

"What have *you* got to say?"

Lorne shrugged. "Nothing."

"I hope you know what you're doing. Do you?"

No comment.

"Who owns these anyway? They're yours, are they? They're not Trevor's? He gave them to you?"

"Dad. . . ."

"What, am I sounding stupid?" He sighed, knowing that the conversation was going nowhere. He stared at his son and nodded his head slightly. "I know, I know," he said. "But when you're the father you got to look at it differently."

A restless silence grew between them. Lorne saw that his father could do with some help. "You had a car when you were eighteen," Lorne said.

"I'd been out working two years by that time."

"Still . . ."

"Sure, we had a few good times in her."

But when he realized that Lorne had made his point, his father's tone changed. "Your mother is really worried about you. I'm worried. You're not working as hard as you used to in school. Your marks are more important than any of this."

"I'll do okay."

"Okay is not good enough. Lorne, you're a smart young fellow. Why let it go to waste? It might be all right for Trevor, he won't be going to university anyway."

"So?"

"That's no answer and you know it. How many times have I wished I had the opportunity you've got now. We've given you everything we could, and I've had to work damn hard to do it. Isn't it about time you showed a little appreciation?"

"I got myself to think about."

"You sure do. So have some sense. Realize what you're doin. Think about your future."

"I do," he answered him. "I think about it all the time."

"God," he said, ready to give up, "I can't figure you out. We never had any of this with Alice."

Twenty-one

To get both the bride and the cluster of girls standing at a distance behind her, Lorne positioned himself on the bandstand, just to the left of the drums. He nodded when he was ready.

As the drumbeat started Shirley raised her bouquet of bright yellow flowers. It uncovered the tight roundness of her stomach. Released from her hand, the flowers sailed over her head. Lorne flashed them in that fraction of a second midway through the air.

They descended at the fringe of the crowd, away from the main throng of outstretched hands. A cheer rang up for the lucky girl. It was Barbara, smiling now, the center of attention. The other girls gathered around, envious of her, several of them kissing her on the cheeks.

"You're next," they kidded. She smiled pleasantly, leading a trail of them laughing back to the table.

"So when's the big day?" one of the girls said to Trevor. He escaped into his beer.

The band stirred again, drawing all eyes back to the dance floor. Shirley was seated in a chair in the center, Hilary kneeling on one knee in front of her. He slipped his hand slowly up her leg, feeling for her garter. His hand lingered there, encouraged by the stream of whistles and catcalls from his buddies gathered at the edge of the floor. She struck him gently on the shoulder, feigning anger, until he had it slipped down and over her foot.

Then it was the single fellows who gathered where the single girls had been before. Another drumroll was struck as Hilary, standing with his back to them, waved the garter over his head. On the final beat he tossed it over his shoulder. Trevor snapped it out of the air. A roar of approval filled the room.

"The two of them. Ay, Trev buddy, you got her now!" someone shouted.

They clamored for Barbara to join him on the floor. Now the person who caught the bouquet had to sit while the person who caught the garter fitted it on her leg. Barbara sat in the chair finally, embarrassed by all the attention.

"So when's the big day?"

"Get out the baby carriage," Hilary called out. Barbara glared at him.

She crossed her legs, the bouquet planted firmly in her lap. Trevor took his time, to the delight of the other fellows. He inched the garter up her leg. Just past the knee he was forced to stop.

"Farther, c'mon, farther. I daresay it's not the first time."

She quickly set her foot to the floor before he had a chance to try it again. She stood up, waited till Trevor got to his feet, then retreated from the dance floor ahead of him, back to her place at the table.

"A jig," they shouted. "A jig. C'mon Melv, get up there." They called for Trevor's father to give them a tune on the accordion, shouting down all his excuses. Finally, when he saw that they were not about to give up, he came forth, speeded unsteadily across the dance floor, and sat on the stool the drummer had set out for him. They handed him the accordion and put a microphone down to his level. He primed it with a scattering of notes, then broke, full tilt, into a rousing jig. Older couples scurried to the dance floor, younger ones not far behind.

They stamped out the rhythm vigorously, then hooked arms in a wild swing. A circle of a dozen couples formed, chasing the music first in one direction and then equally fast in the other. They threw their hands high and gathered to the center, then swept apart to widen the circle once again.

Trevor stood over Barbara, tugging at her hand, urging her to get out on the dance floor with him.

"C'mon," he persisted. "Lorne, you and Elaine get out too."

"Trev, stop it," she said. "I told you no, I don't want to."

He sat down again, cursing her stubbornness.

She pushed away from the table, away from Trevor, and weaved her way through the jumble of tables and chairs to the front entrance.

Trevor was not far behind her. His foot caught the leg of an empty chair. He stumbled but managed to catch himself on one of the tables. He headed out the door.

Lorne ran after him, leaving Elaine at the table. Outside he saw Trevor stumble again and fall to the ground.

"Are you okay?" he said when he reached him.

Trevor let loose a string of curses.

He helped him to his feet. "C'mon back inside."

Trevor tore away from him and headed to the corner of the building, where he found Barbara in the shadows leaning up against it. Lorne turned and walked slowly back toward the main entrance, glancing back over his shoulder several times as he walked.

"What the hell's the matter?" he could hear Trevor shout.

"Nothing." Her voice was barely audible. Lorne had expected her to be crying. She wasn't.

"Don't give me that shit."

"I'll give you any shit I want," she said, her words only slightly louder.

Trevor stood closer to her. "You're crazy," he said.

"And you're drunk," she shouted back.

Trevor banged his fist against the side of the building. "I don't get it. I fuckin don't get it!"

"These flowers, I didn't even want them. They fell into my hands," she declared.

"What?" he said in amazement.

"Trevor, I don't want to end up like that. There's too many things I want to do."

"Who said anything about getting married? I don't

wanna get married, not yet. We can be together without being married, for God's sake."

She didn't say anything.

"You don't even want that."

"I don't know what I want."

He waited for her to say more. She looked away from him, tears starting to form in her eyes.

"The hell with it then. Fuck it!"

He grabbed the flowers from her hands. Stretching his arm back, he fired them as far as he could away from her into the darkness of the trees beyond.

He walked off, leaving her standing there alone.

"Trevor," she called.

He ignored her. He ran past Lorne, who by then had reached the steps. He hauled open the door and stalked back inside.

Twenty-two

The four of them squeezed into the pickup—the three girls and Lorne. He was pinched tight against the door, the handle digging at his leg. To give them all more room he lowered the window and extended his elbow outside. His other arm he rested along the top of the seat behind Elaine and Barbara.

"If he won't come, he won't come," Barbara insisted. "There's nothing I can do that's going to make him change his mind."

"But I can see his point," Lorne said, "can't you?"

"We have to get this interview done," she said. "It's essential to the whole project."

"I almost think we could do without it."

"No way," Gwen warned. "We're taking enough chances as it is."

"And we only got a week left before we have to present it. That doesn't give us much time."

They came in sight of the Senior Citizens Complex. Gwen made a sharp turn onto the road leading to it, sending the weight of the other two girls crushing against Lorne. They hadn't recovered their balance when the front tires thumped into a speed bump and jolted them from their seats, starting a chain of uncontrolled laughter. Gwen stopped the pickup near the end of the building, and their laughter spilled out into the parking lot. It brought several inquisitive faces to the line of apartment windows.

"Shhh," Elaine cautioned, "they're looking at us. They'll think we're crazy."

"Keep it down," Gwen said, "or we'll end up giving them all heart attacks."

As they walked along the concrete toward the front door they burst out laughing again.

A face looked out disapprovingly from the upraised trunk of a car parked near the entrance. It put a sudden stop to their noise. The person was Ryan. He was unloading cardboard boxes, several of which were piled up next to the car.

"Need some help?" Barbara asked with a quick change of expression.

"This is the last of it," he said. "Thank God."

"I guess you never realize how much you have till you start to move," Elaine commented.

They walked closer to the car and gathered up the boxes.

Ryan took the two remaining items, a carton of paperback books and a heavily framed picture, and rested them on the ground while he closed the trunk.

He tried to gather up both of them in his arms, but it proved too awkward. The carton slipped away from him and fell to the ground. He bent down to pick it up again.

"I can carry it," Lorne said.

Ryan ignored him. When the box slipped out of his hands a second time, he moved away from it, embarrassed. "Okay," he said, and walked toward the building carrying only the picture.

He led the way through the front doors. They trailed behind him along the corridor to a door that was slightly ajar. He pushed it inward with his foot, clearing a route directly into the living room.

"Put them down wherever you can find an empty space."

"It's nice," Elaine said, looking around. Most of the furniture seemed to be in place, although all the walls were bare.

"It doesn't have the space I'm used to," Ryan said to her, "but it'll be cheaper to keep up."

He lifted the picture he had brought to a place on the widest wall. The back wire hooked solidly on a nail. The picture was of a boat.

"*The Caribou,*" he informed them. "Sunk by a German U-boat in the Gulf in 1942. A hundred and thirty-seven people lost. My brother was one of them."

The four of them looked at each other, but nobody seemed able to come up with anything appropriate to say.

"The war apparently hasn't got much interest for some of you." He looked at Lorne. "Let's hope you appreciate all the things you *do* have."

It was an uncomfortable start to the visit. Lorne had

purposely hung in the background and let the others
do the talking. Now he felt even more determined to
remain quiet.

Ryan invited them all to sit down. He himself took
what looked to be the most used chair. Barbara
opened the canvas bag she had brought with her and
withdrew a tape recorder. She set it on the arm of the
couch and put her hand back into the bag to retrieve
the cord.

"I don't like tape recorders," he said. "I think you
better just take notes."

"Oh," she said, embarrassed at not having asked his
permission first. She put it back out of sight. Luckily
she had brought a binder with some loose sheets of
paper. She searched in the bag for her pen but
couldn't find it. She cast an inquiring glance at the
others. They shook their heads. Finally Ryan removed
one from his shirt pocket and passed it to her.

"Let's start with what it was like when you first
started teaching," she said with confidence, determined to regain her lost composure.

He gave it what seemed to be considerable thought
before he answered.

"When I came here first it was nothing like what it is
today. The school was a one-room school, and I had
thirty-eight students, seven different grades. No elec-
tricity, no running water. A potbelly stove, and the
students came to school each morning with their junk
of wood."

There was nothing Lorne hadn't heard before. If
not from Ryan, from his grandmother, from his father
and mother. He'd come here for more than this. He
could see it turning into a lecture.

"I came across a picture of the first class I had the other day when I was packing up to move. Let me see if I know where it is."

He searched quickly through a couple of boxes that were not yet unpacked. He found it finally, and sitting back in his chair, he passed it to Barbara.

"That's me on the end."

"You don't look much older than some of the students," Barbara commented.

She passed the photograph along to the other two girls. They looked at it together and gave it then to Lorne.

He stared at the picture unbelievingly. It was the same one he had seen at his grandmother's.

Ryan suddenly walked across the room and withdrew it from his hand. He put the picture away.

He sat back in the chair and continued to talk. Lorne wasn't listening. What is he hiding? Lorne thought. Why didn't his grandmother mention who the teacher was?

In the pause before Barbara's next question Lorne excused himself, saying he'd wait outside in the pickup.

Twenty-three

Lorne wanted them all together backstage for a last-minute meeting.

"We're ready, are we?"

"As ready as we'll ever be."

"Questions?"

There were none.

"Spare bulb for the projector?"

"Got it," Trevor said.

"Lighting okay? Don't forget the change of color on Elaine when she starts to sing."

"Don't worry," Gwen answered.

"And remember," he said, looking at Elaine, "make sure the mike is close enough."

"Calm down, Lorne," Barbara told him. "Hang on to ya ass. You're making us more nervous than we already are."

"Okay, okay, I just want this to be good. We're really going to show him what we can do."

The bell rang outside.

"This is it, b'ys," Trevor summed it up. "Now, remember . . ."

"Remember what?"

"Give er shit."

They made their way to their places, Trevor and Gwen in the back of the auditorium, the other three onstage, behind the curtain. They waited for the audience noise to subside.

Lorne took several deep breaths, well timed so that they ended just before the curtain opened. It revealed a large screen extending to a height of six feet at center stage. Lorne walked out from stage right, Barbara and Elaine from stage left. They sat on the stools and drew the microphones toward themselves.

A concentrated spotlight lit Lorne's head and shoulders.

> "Welcome
>   A welcome strong
>   in verse and song
>   from five graduates
>   who long to offer you
>   a photographic taste
>   of this, our embryonic place
>   our home, our native land.
>
> "Before you, members of our class
>   we'll observe the present
>   survey the past
>   and search to find

> what the future offers
> for us to grasp.
>
> "So, sit back
> relax
> Let the music begin
> and the projector light
> to bring to view the varied sights
> that we call home."

A shout of "Shakespeare lives!" from someone in the audience brought first laughter and then a boisterous round of cheers and applause. Lorne stood up, out of the spotlight, and took a deep, sweeping bow.

A panorama of color filled the screen. It awed the audience to silence. Elaine began to play softly on the guitar as Barbara spoke, pausing after every few lines. Trevor was timing the slide changes perfectly.

> "Perched atop the rocks of Puffin Head
> the camera commands an eagle's view
> of Marten
>
> "And from another rise
> farther down the road
> the sight of Spencer's Harbour unfolds.
>
> "These two are lapped
> by the same Atlantic tide
>
> "that from the other side
> brought our ancestral folk.

"From west country England
  with nets they came

"in search of yet
  more of the abundant cod

"to catch and split
  gut, salt, and spread
  out on the flakes to dry.

"And settling here
  they labored hard and long
  fishing, sealing, farming

"recording both in heart and song
  their struggle to survive."

Here Elaine added the traditional words of "Hard,
Hard Times" to her guitar music as old pictures drawn
from history books continued to fade in and out on the
screen. Her voice plaintively filled the auditorium.
When she finished, Lorne picked up the narration.

"From the wood
  that in profusion stood nearby

"they built their homes
  their schools and churches.

"They worked the scanty soil
  that through hard toil
  produced what vegetables it could.

"Their lot was meager, humble
 but not, in spite of all,
 without its moments of delight

"For in between
 the new year and the old
 lingered twelve days of Christmas cheer

"when one would hear
 the sounds of mummering fun
 enhanced by a scattered taste
 of black Jamaican rum."

Before Lorne finished speaking, Trevor had let the projector light fade out. He rushed as inconspicuously as he could out of the room and around to the back entrance of the stage, just in time to whip up the accordion and start the music. Barbara and Elaine were still dragging themselves into their mummer disguises, one in mismatched remnants of dresses and underwear, the other in the scruffy oversize clothes of a rubber-booted old man. They draped lace curtain over their faces and hauled on old hats to keep it in place.

The music sped them out to wild roars and hand-clapping from the audience. Trevor's playing, while lacking polish, was enough to keep them lively. Hands on their hips, they step-danced face-to-face, then back and forth to the front of the stage, all inhibitions lost in their disguises.

When once again the stage was bare, Lorne resumed his place at the microphone. Color again filled

the screen, bringing the audience back to its former
silence.

"And now, today
  as the camera scans the wide array
  of scenes upon our shores

"we see the range of changes
  brought by modern life.

"A tower beams television dreams
  An asphalt road leads
  out the cove
  to a bigger cove beyond.

"The cod remain, of course
  plus new gain from lobster
  herring, capelin
  and tourists too.

"This new fish plant stands
  as long promised
  with unsteady jobs for the workingman.

"Yet the communities cannot bear the weight
  and it's many a graduate's fate each year
  to be heading west
  to Toronto or to Calgary
  which already holds a store of refugees
  cast there
  by the same economic fate
  that we so ignobly await.

> "What answers then we ask
>   for survival when at last
>   we graduate?"

Now three of them were standing across the stage, having raised the height of each microphone. A voice grew at each one.

Barbara spoke first, her voice aged and quivering slightly, suggesting an old woman:

> "Foolish! Foolish altogether, the way of life to-day. No peace to it, no order to it. When I was growing up, if you had a quarter or a dollar you'd think you had a fortune. Now the young ones can't get enough money to satisfy em. They got to learn to live on less, that's all there is to it. And find out what work is. We had to work, I can tell you—raising sheep, pigs, cows, tendin the gardens, spreading the fish. We were used to it. But if what's around growin up today had to work like the ones before em had to do, I daresay they wouldn't last a week."

Lorne, in the speech of an educated man, added further comment:

> "Times have changed. The economic system is altogether different. There's a way out of all this unemployment if the government would just take time to stop and think about it. Make every young fellow leaving school give two years of service in the armed forces. Build up this country's defenses, which are in a shambles as it is, and get those young people off the streets at the same

time. They need something to straighten them out. I put in time in the army, I served in the war. It was one of the most worthwhile experiences I ever had in my life."

The spotlight switched to Elaine, now a middle-aged woman, her quiet role in contrast to the others:

"Take advantage of all the opportunities you have. Stay in school, go to university, get your education. I just wish I'd had that chance when I was growing up. You can't go wrong by going to university. When the jobs are scarce it's those with the least education who are going to suffer most. Put your mind to it when you're young, and you won't be regretting it when you're older—"

Lorne, as a teenager, broke in:

"Ah, enjoy yourself while you're young. Half that comes out of university now can't find a job. Why slave your guts out, you're only going this way once. Find work enough so's you can draw your unemployment, and then the hell with it. As long as you got enough money for a car and a good tear now and then, what more do you want? When you're married, that's time enough to worry about a steady job—"

Elaine, with stiffened stance, interrupted:

"Steady job? There'll be plenty of steady jobs when this off-shore oil goes on stream. When will that be? Five years? Ten years? No, you're right, you can't sit around and wait for it. But it's com-

ing. Just keep this government in office. We'll be
one of the 'have' provinces yet. Wait and see.''

Barbara, in the most solemn, most distressed of the
voices, silenced them all:

"I don't think it matters much what you do. The
way things are going now, we might all be blown
off the face of the earth soon anyway. All it takes is
for someone to press the button. One thing for
sure, if there is a nuclear war, we'll all be better off
dead.''

The other two withdrew in silence, leaving Lorne
with the last word.

> "The ring, the clatter
>   free advice
>   from those who've made their choices.
>   History has said its peace.
>
> "But the future of which we speak
>   is ours, not theirs
>   the mistakes we make
>   what decisions we take at last
>   belong not to the past. . . .
>   They belong to us.''

He stepped back as the spotlight faded and the curtain closed.

Wild applause filled the auditorium.

A short while later when Lorne and the others
emerged from backstage, they saw the audience being
hurried back to the classroom. Several of the students

shouted their congratulations. Barnes and some others stuck up their thumbs to them.

The five of them, ignoring Ryan and his attempt to clear the auditorium, raised their hands above their heads triumphantly, half in jest, half in defiance.

Twenty-four

As Elaine and Lorne watched, Trevor kicked off his
sneakers and brushed them into a corner with his foot.
He yelled out twice to Barbara. An unintelligible answer filtered from a distant part of the house. He
strolled up the four steps to the living room, a beer
bottle held inside his jean jacket. By the time Barbara
appeared, he had slumped into one of the plush
armchairs.

"Thought I'd drop in to see ya," he said to her. He
smiled broadly; then, when she responded with a less
than pleasant look, he stared apologetically into her
eyes.

Elaine and Lorne, less bold, lingered at the foot of
the stairs. When Barbara realized they were there, she
went over and motioned for them to come into the

living room. "There's no one home, just me and Keith," she told them.

"We weren't sure," Lorne explained. "We didn't wanna just barge in."

"Friday nights they always go out," Trevor yelled. "I told you that."

Once in the living room, Lorne found a place on the carpet. Elaine sat on the sofa near Barbara.

"I'd like to have my hands around his goddamn throat!" Trevor announced. "What a prick, b'y. A lousy *D*."

"It was supposed to be a history presentation, he says, not a song and dance. Not enough detail!" Lorne added, his disgust just as strong.

"The other teachers who saw it liked it. Langman said he thought it was great."

"It's Ryan's way of getting back at us. It's not fair!"

"It's my fault," Lorne said. "I'm the one who insisted we make it different."

"But we all agreed to it," Elaine pointed out.

"It was that bit about the army that really did us in."

"Wait till graduation. He's got another surprise coming yet. I've still got a valedictory to give," Lorne said.

Trevor sank deeper in his chair. "Graduation. That's another laugh. What chance have I got of passing?"

"Forget it," Lorne said. "The school mark is only worth fifty percent. The provincial exam'll bring your mark up."

"Fat fuckin chance."

Barbara's twelve-year-old brother came down from

upstairs and walked into the room. He carried a book by his side, his finger stuck between the pages.

Trevor looked at him. "Keith, want a beer?"

He shook his head. "No, thanks. Can you help me with this question?" he said to his sister. "We're doing this section on the eye."

"Come here, then."

Keith walked across the room toward Barbara. Trevor planted his foot on the coffee table to block his path.

"C'mon," Trevor said, "sit down and take it easy. Go out in the car and get yourself a beer."

"I wanna get this done."

Trevor extended his other leg and locked the two in a scissors hold around Keith's waist.

"Trev."

"Put down the book." He squeezed hard. "C'mon, drop it."

"Ow!"

"Trev, you're hurting him," Barbara said, raising her voice.

"Don't talk so foolish."

Keith was powerless. The book fell from his hands as he tried in vain to get loose.

"Take it easy for a while. Fuck the science questions, old man. It's Friday night."

"Leave me alone."

"Trevor, let him go." Barbara's face tensed, her lips pressed against each other.

Keith, picking up on his sister's hint of temper, swung his fists wildly at Trevor. One swing caught him roughly on the corner of the mouth.

Keith stopped, surprised by what he'd done. Trevor loosened his legs and put them back to the floor.

"Watch it," Trevor said, his hand to his face, the trace of humor gone from his voice.

"Serves you right," Barbara said carelessly.

Trevor sat up straight in the chair, anger smoldering inside him. Keith moved away.

"Wimp," Trevor called out as Keith left the room.

"Leave him alone. What the hell's wrong with you. Can't he make up his own mind about anything?"

The sharpness of her words hurt him deeply.

"Ah, get off my back, will ya," he yelled at her.

She stared at him. Her silence was all the apology she was willing to give. Lorne and Elaine glanced at each other uncomfortably.

"Well, screw you, if that's the way you feel." He jumped up. "And this time it's for good."

He walked out of the room. Lorne followed him to the top of the stairs. He looked down on him as he forced his feet into his sneakers. "Trev, you sure you should be driving?"

He opened the door. "Watch me," he said, and slammed it shut.

Twenty-five

He walked noiselessly down the stairs to where his father was working. He could see him at the desk under a beam of concentrated light, the only light in the room. He was bent forward, tying salmon flies.

"Mom said you wanted to see me," he said quietly.

"Sit down. There's a chair."

"Is it going to take that long?"

"C'mon," he said, "sit down."

The empty chair had obviously been planted near the desk. Lorne sat in it.

"I should show you how to do this sometime. It's a great way to spend your spare time, if you ever get into salmon fishing."

"Sure," he said.

"You should make a trip up the river with me this

year," his father said with a cautious measure of enthusiasm. He turned to him for his response. "After you finish exams."

Lorne didn't say anything.

"In fact, that's what I've been thinking about for a graduation present—a salmon fishing rod. The real good ones are expensive, but they're worth it if you do any amount of fishing at all."

"Sure."

"You don't sound very interested."

Lorne's expression remained unchanged except for a slight twist of his mouth.

"I just thought we could do some fishing together. You'd rather another piece of camera equipment? You could get some great pictures up the river."

"You don't have to get me anything."

"I know I don't."

They stared at each other for a few seconds, until Lorne made a move to leave. "I better go."

"Wait a minute."

"I've got something I've got to get done."

"Sit down," his father said with a sharpness that surprised both of them.

Lorne slipped back slowly from the edge of the chair.

"I just want to talk to you. I'm not asking much," he said almost apologetically.

"Sorry," Lorne said quickly.

"What's all the rush about anyway?" he asked, to give them both a chance to settle back.

"I'm working on the valedictory for next week."

"The valedictory? For the graduation? That's great.

You never told me you were picked to do that. Alice gave the valedictory speech at her graduation."

"I know."

"Did you tell your mother?"

"I haven't got around to it yet."

"She could use a little good news. She's been awful upset about you."

"She worries too much. She always makes such a fuss about everything."

"Perhaps she do. But give her a chance. You haven't been very nice to her lately."

Lorne made no comment.

"That's not the only reason I wanted you to come down."

Lorne waited, having moved his arms about until he had finally folded them.

"There's something I've been meaning to tell you for a while. I put it off," he said. "It's got to do with your grandmother." He looked directly at his son. "Did you know she went to school to Mr. Ryan at one time?"

It was obvious that his father thought he had made a great revelation. Lorne let the question settle before replying. "I had an idea that she did. I saw some pictures."

His answer caught his father unprepared. He was silent for a moment, but then he continued. "There's a bit more to it than that. It was the first year he taught, the year before he went overseas. They had sort of a . . . well, they were seeing each other, going out together. Apparently not many people knew about it."

Lorne covered his surprise as best he could.

"And . . . from what people have told me . . .

they were thinking about getting married when he came back from overseas."

"What happened?"

"Your grandfather started seeing her. He convinced her she should put Mr. Ryan out of her mind and that the two of them should get married."

"And when the war was over?"

"He showed up. She hadn't told him."

There was a period when neither of them spoke.

"He went away. He worked at other things, but in the end he went to college, and he came back here to teach again. I don't think your grandfather ever resented that. He and your grandmother had a good life together. They were happy enough. They had five of us to look after."

It was a lot to take in at one time. His father was looking for his reaction.

"Is that supposed to change things between him and me?"

"Think about it," his father said.

"I don't think it should. If I'm honest, I don't think it should."

He left the room as quietly as he had entered it.

His father sat motionless in the chair for a long while. Then, reaching forward, he shut off the light.

Twenty-six

Elaine's brother dropped them off at McDonald's on Kenmount Road. They would eat first and then shop before catching the 5:30 bus that would take them as far as the Marten turnoff.

He glutted himself on Quarter Pounders and the largest size Coke. Elaine picked at a few french fries.

"That won't keep you going all afternoon," he told her, and made her drink half his Coke. "I'll order another one."

"Lorne, you'll be too bloated to walk. We'll get something later." He ignored what she said and went back to the counter.

He loved it, being in St. John's, out on his own like that, in a new environment where nobody knew him. He felt he'd like to stay there for a week.

Elaine was right, it had been too much. As they walked toward Avalon Mall it seemed as if his guts were going to burst. He let out a thunderous belch.

"Lord, what a pig." She ran ahead as if he had disgusted her.

He ran after her but stopped after a few steps, rubbing his stomach and groaning. She couldn't stop laughing at him.

The laughter was contagious. "Oh, shit," he said, "don't make me laugh. It makes it worse. Don't," he moaned. "Elaine, don't."

The afternoon was so rushed, he said it reminded him of the speeded action of a silent movie. They hurried their way through the mall, store by store, one trying on clothes while the other leaned against the wall outside the fitting room. They weren't sure exactly what they were looking for but each time they knew they hadn't found it.

In an open area of the mall they discovered a booth where people were having their portraits taken in turn-of-the-century clothing. Without a second thought they decided they'd have it done. From the racks of costumes they chose outfits and put them on over their street clothes. Elaine posed in a full-length red satin gown trimmed in wide ruffles of black lace, with a broad-brimmed feather hat and parasol to match. Lorne stood beside her, equally solemn, in a black vested suit, complete with pocket watch, bowler hat, and cane.

The picture, tinted brown and in an ornate plastic frame, delighted them, especially Lorne. "Instant history," he explained. "It's great."

By mid-afternoon he found a suit that appealed to

them enough that he settled on buying it. But Elaine still hadn't found anything she liked. She dragged him from book and camera stores to catch a bus to the shopping area downtown. On Water Street they continued the search, and finally she tried on a dress that they both agreed was the one.

"You're not just saying that because you're sick of looking?" she said, turning in front of the mirror.

"No," he retorted with exaggerated delight, "you'll look great at the graduation. Sort of elegant, but not too elegant."

"But elegant enough for a really expensive corsage, right?" she said, smiling.

They had a half hour to spare before it was time to catch the bus for home. In a nearby restaurant they ordered a couple of sandwiches. They talked over coffee as they waited for the sandwiches to arrive.

"I hate that stupid bus," he said. "It takes so long."

"You should be able to sleep."

"Wanna stay overnight and go back in the morning?" he asked in a tone of voice so casual it surprised even him.

She laughed.

"We'll phone home and tell them we missed the bus," he added quickly.

"You're crazy," she said, not sure now if he were joking.

"I'm serious."

He searched her face for an answer. Her mind still hadn't had time to deal fully with what he was asking.

"Where would we stay?"

"I've got money," he said. "I'll ask your brother to cover for us. We'll say we stayed at his apartment."

She still couldn't answer his inquiring gaze.

"I've got protection."

"Lorne." He had forced her to look away.

He realized then that he had jumped into it too quickly. "I'm sorry. It's okay," he said. "It was only a suggestion."

But she could see that he wasn't really backing away. He was only giving her more time. There was a long, leaden silence.

"Not this time," she said finally. "I need more time to think about it. It's too sudden."

In one sense he felt relieved. He had got through it without looking stupid. He would have been surprised if she had said yes. But neither had she dismissed it outright. It was a significant step closer.

On the bus back they had a longer talk. The high-backed seats and the noise of the bus provided a strangely intimate setting. Their day together had injected a new frankness into their conversation.

The thing he most wanted to know was her feeling now about Ryan. "For sure," he said, "you've been thinking about it. You can't feel so sorry for him anymore."

"In a way I do."

"Ah, c'mon."

"I do."

"You know what he did wasn't fair."

He told her what his father had told him. She looked at him, amazed.

"And it still makes no difference," he said. "I still think he's a jerk."

"And you're going to get back at him."

"The valedictory will have something to say about it."

"In front of all those people? You're only going to make it worse. Revenge is just as bad as what he did."

"He deserves it."

"The difference is I can forgive him and you can't," she said. "Right?"

"Why should I?"

"It would make things a lot easier."

"Perhaps too easy?" he asked.

Twenty-seven

In the gymnasium metallic streamers radiated from a high central point to form a shimmering canopy over the banquet tables, a huge cluster of balloons suspended through its apex. On the wall behind the head table, crepe-paper flowers shaped the words "Don't Give Up on a Dream." Four long tables stretched perpendicularly from the head table, halfway down the length of the gym. There were place settings for more than a hundred and fifty people.

A wall of vertical streamers separated the banquet area from the rest of the gym; a rectangular wooden archway outlined with flowers was the only entrance to the inside. The crowd, waiting for the announcement to enter, mingled about noisily.

When Langman paused for a second on his way

inside to say hello to Lorne and Elaine, Lorne's father introduced himself.

"You can be very proud of your son," Langman told him.

"Thank you."

"It's a pleasure to teach someone who's got a mind of his own."

"He takes after his father for that," Lorne's mother said.

Langman continued on his way into the banquet area. "Got to set up the microphone," he said. "Talk to you later."

"He seems like a very nice man," his mother said to Lorne.

Lorne, his mind on something else, agreed.

Graduates and their guests and parents gathered from time to time under the archway to have their pictures taken. Lorne's father had brought his Polaroid. He insisted on a photograph of Lorne and Elaine, even though he knew Lorne hated having anyone take his picture. The two stood together under the archway while his father moved closer, then farther back, trying to decide the best position.

"Take the picture," Lorne said impatiently. "There are other people waiting."

He pressed the shutter release, producing a flash and a loud whir as the potential picture advanced out the front of the camera.

"Wait," Elaine said to Lorne, "stay there. I'll take one of you with your father and mother."

His parents thought the idea wonderful. They gathered around him before he could come up with a way out of it.

"Everyone smile."

He reacted with the others on cue, speeding up the whole process as much as he could. He walked away from them with the flash still spotting in his eyes.

A lowering of the noise level in the room made them decide to stay in the vicinity of the archway. They stood together with Elaine's parents in anticipation of an announcement being made, in the meantime passing around the pictures as they continued to develop. The noise level rose again as if everyone had become too conscious of the quiet.

When Lorne looked around to see why, he drew back as if someone had suddenly waved something before his face. He was struck with an image he could not comprehend. Walking toward them, together as a couple, were Ryan and his grandmother.

His father welcomed them into the group, showing no surprise at their being together. Lorne looked at Elaine, who shared his shocked silence.

"You're just in time," Lorne's father told them. "Stand over there now and I'll take your picture."

The old woman, aware that most people in the room were continuing to look at them, resisted the suggestion.

"I'm willing, Muriel," Ryan said. "That would make it official. Maybe then they'd stop staring."

She reluctantly agreed. They moved into the empty space under the archway.

"Make what official?" Lorne asked his mother in a whisper.

"What do you think? They're planning to get married."

His father gave Lorne the picture to hold while it

developed. He stared at it in disbelief. Their obscure shapes, ghostlike, gradually took form before his eyes into hard, indiscriminate detail. They looked happy to be together. He could not draw his eyes from the picture.

Only when Ryan spoke to him was he forced to face them. "I suppose," he was being asked, "a future relative could get a good price on a wedding photographer."

Lorne's awkward search for a response was answer enough for them. They turned away from him to the announcement of the head-table guests.

Inside, seated with his parents and across from Elaine and her parents, he was unable to enjoy his meal. He scrutinized his speech, first from memory and then, as the time drew closer, from the written text he took from the inside pocket of his new suit. His pen he left where it was. The impression would be that he was doing no more than reading it over.

When he did get up to speak, he gave the speech everybody had come to expect from valedictorians. He thanked teachers and parents and said that as graduates they had achieved only one goal. He referred to dreams and to their future lives. Flashbulbs exploded in his face and made it difficult to look relaxed.

He ended rather too quickly, they all thought, with a quote Elaine had passed to him under the table: "Your old men shall dream dreams, your young men shall see visions." They did seem especially pleased that the quotation had come from the Bible.

Twenty-eight

He smoked a spliff of hash oil with Trevor on the way down in the car. The roach burnt his lip, but he said he couldn't have cared less. When Trevor parked the car near the path through the woods, he grabbed one of the cases of beer and slammed the door shut.

Elaine followed behind him with a flashlight, lighting the way until they came in sight of the fire. The beach was already crowded with people standing around the fire, laughing, drinking, watching the fire shoot sparks high into the black sky. They found a spot for themselves and the beer.

Trevor took the liter bottle of wine. He tore away the foil and twisted loose the wire cage. With his thumbs he pressed against the plastic. It failed to move until, applying even more pressure, he slowly worked it upward. It burst out with a sudden pop, shot through the sparks, and arched away out of sight. They cheered loudly and passed the bottle from mouth to mouth.

> Then . . . later
> we raced for the water
> there was no other way
> and no turning back
> once we had begun
> no stopping
> even after
> the first brush
> against the surface
> had bitten the nerve ends
> of our feet.
>
> I skimmed the shallow part
> straight-faced
> determined to keep up
> the sprinter's pace
> then splashing through
> I cut in and out
> in ever wilder leaps
> until the thigh-deep water
> broke my speed
> and balance
> leaving me no choice
> but to dive headlong
> into the water
> into the ICE COLD Atlantic waters
> my breath held just long enough . . .
> till I could stand it no more

and burst
the surface
to shout! and yell!
out the pain.

And . . .
as if thinking it were possible
to get any wetter
we began to thrust
the heels of our hands
against the surface
driving water
with new force
into each other's face.

He raced back at that
For an agonizing moment
I floated toward shore
face up
mouth wide open
until I could stand it no more
and bolted clear of the water
chasing my senses
back onto the land.

They rushed to the intense heat of the fire to thaw themselves. They were both shivering madly, their hair cold matted clumps, their reddened gooseflesh dripping water.

Elaine borrowed blankets to cover them. She helped them to rub dry.

"You two are crazy," she said. "You'll have pneumonia."

"Fuck the pneumonia," Lorne declared, still shivering.

In the darkness nearby they discarded their wet underwear and changed back into dry clothes. By the fire again, they cleaned their feet of sand as best they could and held them to the heat until it penetrated the iciness and they hauled them back, almost burnt.

Fully dressed, they still shivered. The three of them sat in the sand near the fire. Trevor stared at it as Elaine and Lorne curled tightly together. Finally he stood up with his beer in his hand. He tossed Lorne the keys to his car without saying a word and walked away.

"Where's he goin?" Elaine asked.

"To look for Barbara?"

Twenty-nine

He said that he needed to get warmer. They found their way back up the path to Trevor's car, she helping him to his feet when he stumbled. Once in the front seat he quickly started the engine and turned on the heater. Elaine lowered the side window a fraction of an inch.

He was able finally to control his shivering, enough that he turned down the rearview mirror and combed his hair. He smoothed down the sparse hair on his upper lip with his fingers, then put his arm around Elaine, drawing her to him. With his other hand he fiddled with the radio until he found some music they both liked. The car had been going long enough that he could now turn the heater on full blast. Warm air surged up from under the dash.

He closed his eyes and kissed her spiritedly, trying to be tender but getting lost in it for too long. When he drew back he looked at her more boldly than he had ever done before. Returning to her lips, he undid her coat and moved his hand up to her breast. She squirmed momentarily but did not resist. His hand slid under her sweater and found a way to her bra. He smoothed the satiny roundness for a few seconds and moved his hand excitedly along the strap to search for the clasp. With some difficulty he was able to undo it.

His hand curved to enclose her bare breast. His heartbeat quickened. He stroked it, his fingers brushing against the hardness of the nipple. He began to massage it with quick pulsations of his palm and fingers.

They sank to a horizontal position along the seat, his arm a rigid pillow for her head. One knee on the hump of the floor helped to support his weight. Heat rushed into their faces, suffocating them, so he withdrew his hand and clumsily searched until it found the heater switch. He nestled his face into the curve of her neck.

His hand now rested at the waistband of her jeans, his heart pounding with the noisy vibration of the car. He undid the metal button and for the first time she showed resistance. He stopped for a second but slowly renewed his efforts. In a deliberately quick motion he slid down the zipper.

She twisted her body in protest. The message was clear. Nevertheless, his hand wandered inside her jeans.

"Lorne," she said in anger now.

He yielded to the pressure of her hand against his.

"Lorne," she said again, with only slightly less anger, "please get up."

He sat up behind the steering wheel, while she straightened her clothes and sat up at the far end of the seat.

"I'm sorry," he said.

She didn't answer him.

"You had a right to get mad."

"You think I'm really a prude."

"No, I don't."

"Did you want to do it because you like me or just to say you could do it? Would you have tried it if you hadn't been drinking all night?"

"Elaine."

"No, I'm serious. That's all you've had on your mind, isn't it?"

"No, it isn't."

"I can't say I believe you."

"Then don't." Now he was the one mad.

She stared at him. "Lorne, it just didn't feel right to me. It was like you set me up for this. I don't know . . . you're trying too hard to act like you think fellows should be acting, trying to be too much like Trevor or something."

He didn't want to hear any of it. "You're making too much of it. I said I was sorry . . . let's leave it at that."

"Lorne?"

"I don't want to talk about it anymore, okay?" he said, raising his voice to her for the first time. "I can't handle anymore of this right now."

"Why can't we talk about it? Where do you keep your feelings anyway, in your poetry somewhere?"

He kept quiet.

"I just don't want us to go away mad at each other," she said, softly now.

She moved her hand toward his, which was lying beside him on the seat. She held on to it tightly.

"Perhaps you've had too much to drink."

"Good God, stop it, will ya. You're sounding like my mother or something."

Thirty

On his way back from walking Elaine home he stopped at the machine outside the service station and deposited the money for a soft drink. The can clanged down through the machine to the slot below, the noise shattering the emptiness of the night. Air hissed into the can as he forced in the metal tab.

Out of habit he looked at the wrist where his watch used to be. He thought it must be about three A.M. He walked farther up the empty road until he came in sight of the school. He found a dark enough spot against somebody's fence and sat down on the damp grass.

Just what did she expect from him? Love. He supposed he loved her. Did he want to do it because he loved her? Or was it just the satisfaction of knowing that he could, to have it over with? He didn't know.

He knew one thing—he didn't want to have to think about it right now. He wanted to forget it, free himself to enjoy the rest of the night. There should be enough of a party left to make up for what had happened.

He walked up the road, back in the direction of the beach. A car passed him going the other way. He held up his hand to them; the driver blew the horn. He hoped the party wasn't over.

When he reached the field where Trevor's car had been parked, he saw that it was no longer there. He decided to try the couple of tents that had been set up at the end of the field, to see if he could find out where Trevor had gone.

Trevor's tent had the front flap open, as if someone had just left in a hurry. Lorne stuck his head inside, expecting it to be empty.

He was met with a startled voice and the sudden glare of a flashlight in his eyes. "God, what a fright."

Lorne got just as big a scare. He knew instantly that it was Gwen.

"I didn't know who the hell it could be," she said, moving the light away from his face.

"You see Trevor?" he asked.

"He's gone on down to the point to find somebody with cigarettes." She sat up, a sleeping bag bundled around her. "You goin to wait for him?"

It was definitely an invitation. One that this time he would accept without thinking much about it.

He sat inside on the other sleeping bag, which was spread across the floor of the tent.

"Close the flap," she said, "it's freezin in here."

He did so with the help of the flashlight.

"He'll probably be gone for a while," she said.

She lay back on a layer of foam.

She turned off the flashlight. He felt his limbs turn rigid as if touched unexpectedly from behind. At least this time there was darkness to hide any uneasiness he was feeling.

The sound of her breathing invited him closer. There was no way he would retreat from this. He talked himself into a sense of calm, near confidence.

He removed his coat and spread himself lengthwise in a position he thought must be alongside her. He felt for her body next to his.

Relax, he thought, and let things happen. Nobody knows anything. She wrapped the sleeping bag around them both, forcing him closer. One of his arms found a place under her head. The other approached her body.

He discovered her naked except for her jeans. His hand smoothed her skin as gently as it could. He kissed her hard on the mouth, his eyes daringly wide but unseeing. She moved his hand to touch her breasts. He was surprised to find them smaller than he had expected. He played with them, moving his hand from one to the other.

His hand curved around and down her back to the waistband of her jeans. Its looseness told him the front was already undone. He slipped his fingers inside and felt her rear cold as ice.

He discovered he could laugh at that without insulting her.

Her joking response made him bolder. He opened the front of his own jeans and with relief, then delight, confirmed the stirrings inside. He forced down his clothes, releasing his penis, confident that it could only get stiffer.

She felt for it, encouraged it. It turned as hard and anxious as it had ever been. He helped her get out of her jeans. She moved her legs apart and, holding it in her hand again, she rubbed the head against herself. His whole body stiffened in pleasure. He thrust forward.

"Wait," she said.

He remembered. "I've got one in my pocket."

He searched his pockets and found it still there. He withdrew his arm from under her head and, lying on his back, he tore open the pouch. All the while she stroked him faster and faster. He rushed against time.

Just as he had it out of the pouch, he heard a car, far off but approaching. The noise it made left no doubt.

"Trevor," she said.

"Shit." He sighed.

She hesitated, stopped for a second, then continued to stroke him, harder and even faster now. He lay back beyond control. In a few seconds it surged out over the thick wool of his sweater.

There was no moment of calm, only a hurried movement apart. They stormed back into their clothes.

Thirty-one

Before he sat down, Lorne tossed on several small sticks to revive the fire. He lay back on the sand, his head against a log, his hands folded on his stomach, near the spot where he and Elaine had sat earlier. He was the only one left at the fire. The few that had not yet gone for the night were out on the rocks nearer the shore waiting for the sun to rise. The flame of the fire, when it rose, reddened his face.

He could not remember ever staying awake till dawn. He was determined to see it through. One more thing to be recalled.

He was exhausted, yet brimming with answers.

> A dawning breathes fire
> having extinguished desire

with a well-tried attempt
at experience due

But let not the difference
between love feigned and innocent
lay there unnoticed
blocking the view

Nor let your survival
depend on the tribal
the ways of the father
needn't be the son's too

For all I request
is a try at my best
at making the most
of what I can do

When Trevor showed up, the fire was blazing again. He sat in the sand and took out a cigarette, using a smoldering stick from the edge of the fire to light it. He passed the stick along to Lorne, who used it to light one himself.

"That's the best light you can get. You get the flavor of the wood coming right through."

Lorne tossed it back to the fire. "You carry her home?" he asked.

"Finally. What a friggin time I had tryin to get rid of her." He took another draw of his cigarette. "She's not exactly shy, that's for sure."

It brought a smile from Lorne.

"Is she?" Trevor said, grinning. "You must know.

You weren't outta breath from talking about the weather."

Lorne offered guarded laughter.

"Hell, it didn't bother me, old man. I had her primed for you. I was only at it for a laugh, the same as you."

Their laughter let loose together, loud and carefree.

But when it died away, Lorne was left with his old expression. "I don't know," he said after a while. "It's Elaine. We had this stupid argument."

It produced a sudden mellowing in Trevor. "Welcome to the club."

"I can't get it out of my mind."

"They start to take everything so fuckin serious," Trevor said. "You feel like, I don't know, saying the hell with them."

"I know."

"But you keep wanting things to be like they were before the fight. I really like her a lot. I'm trying to make myself believe it shouldn't bug me. Shit, we went together for two years," Trevor said. "Makes you wanna fuck off somewhere, away from everything."

"Another few months," Lorne said, "and I'm going anyway."

"University?"

"Somewhere."

"I don't know what I'm going to do. Fish with the old man for the summer. After that, I don't know. He's after me to try to get into Fisheries College. But my marks probably won't even get me through this year. I'd like to find a job in the fall. Hilary says things have slowed down up there a lot, so I daresay I'll end up home at the squids and hope I get enough weeks to draw my unemployment."

With that he tossed the butt of his cigarette into the fire.

"Ah, fuck it," he said, "I still got the car. There's still a few good laughs left yet."

Thirty-two

The sign said it was against the law to even be inside the fence, but that didn't stop Trevor, or Lorne from following him. Trevor said he had been on top twice before.

The water tower stood on a base of four legs and rose fifty or sixty feet off the ground, near a pond along one of the back roads. A series of six vertical ladders ran from just above ground level to the walkway that surrounded the reservoir itself.

At one point Lorne did look down. For some reason, whether it was the weak light just before sunrise or the remnants of the courage he had been feeling all night, it didn't bother him as much as he had thought it might. He increased his pace almost enough to keep up with Trevor.

Only when he climbed in over the railing did the full impact of the height strike him. He leaned back hard against the tank's wooden casing. Trevor accused him of being too nervous to even take a picture. He denied it vigorously and spit over the railing as joking proof. He uncovered his camera and snapped a quick picture.

"Of course I'm shitbaked, you jerk. Hurry up and get it over with."

With his gloved hand Trevor retrieved a spray can of bright yellow paint from inside his jacket. Stretching up to start each letter and ending it three feet below, he gradually formed his notice to the world: GRADUATED, EH? At the end of the question mark he tossed the can nonchalantly over his shoulder.

On the ground again, they stood back from the base and admired the results of their escapade.

"Fan-fuckin-tastic!"

Once off and running, they smacked each other on the back to salute their success. They followed a route through the woods to where the car was parked.

They were riding a newfound crest of energy. The car sped through Marten, slowing only briefly to go around a pickup backing out of a driveway. The early morning was bringing out fishermen on their way to their boats.

Trevor figured they might as well take a run to Spencer's before finding their way back to the tent and crashing out. Lorne agreed.

"No cops," Trevor reasoned.

A Springsteen song about a father surfaced above the noise of the car. Lorne turned up the volume until it filled their ears. He kept time aimlessly on his leg; his mouth urgently formed the words. He closed his eyes.

When he opened them again the car had topped the hill and was heading straight down the grade toward the wharf. Lorne smiled at the thought that Trevor must be trying to scare him. Trevor laughed and drove the brake pedal to the floor. The fun exploded into fear.

The brakes failed.

The car, the two of them inside, terrified, struck the winch at the end of the wharf. The impact crushed Trevor's face into the steering wheel, smashing a smileful of teeth to bloody stumps. His nose flattened into his face, his forehead butted metal, draping him senseless over the steering wheel before the car hit the water.

Lorne, stunned, remained conscious despite the crash of his head against the windshield.

Seawater immediately enclosed the car. It gushed in through the hole left by the broken windshield, sweeping pebbles of broken glass against Lorne's face.

As the water filled the inside he hauled at Trevor's arm in a maddening effort to drag him away from the steering wheel and out through the front with him. His breathing was forced to a stop in mid-breath. He struggled between fright for his own life and his determination to free his friend. Finally he had to give up, and he pushed out through the opening in hope of finding the surface.

His head jerked clear of water. He sputtered for air. There were empty boats floating within ten feet of him. He struggled to one, his face sinking under the water time after time.

Minutes later the same fisherman they had passed on the road showed up and found him clinging to the boat for his life.

"He's still in the car!" Lorne raged at him.

Thirty-three

Trevor's face, when they finally got him to the surface, was a picture of horror. He wished it were like the pictures of wars and massacres that could be put away or closed over or looked at knowing that another more pleasant picture would take its place. The image creased his mind; it would never fade. Trevor was dead.

They had to force Lorne into the pickup to drive him to the hospital. He shivered uncontrollably despite the coats they wrapped around him and the heat blasting up from under the dash.

He said nothing all the way into Bakerton. The fellow driving tried to get him to talk, but he only nodded inattentively.

What had he faced? The senselessness of it all

bound him to a numb silence. His mind screamed to escape. He felt an acute tightness on his forehead, as if his brain were pressuring his skull. He pressed his hand against the spot and felt a hard swelling and the torn edge of his skin. Blood drained onto his fingertips. He smeared it across his wet jeans.

He knew nothing from his past that he could measure against it, no tragedy ever this bad, nothing that promised understanding of it or recovery. He needed to be warm and wrapped in a love that would not ask questions.

They kept him in the hospital for observation and confined him to bed. Minutes after the doctor had gone, his mother and father arrived in the room. They found him staring aimlessly, his forehead covered by a wide bandage.

His mother cried when he looked at her. Tears wet his face as she kissed him and clung to him. His arms held her tightly.

When he released her, his father held his hand. He told Lorne that he was not to talk, that he should rest.

"It wasn't his fault," Lorne said urgently. "It was nobody's fault."

His father insisted that they believed him.

"The brakes gave out. He tried to stop. He wasn't drunk."

"It doesn't matter, Lorne. We can talk about it later."

When they said they would leave for a while to let him rest, he insisted that they stay. He did not want to be alone, he needed them. Only later, when Elaine came in the room, did they go and look for the doctor.

Elaine stroked his face with her cold fingers, then rested her hand on his.

"You're going to be okay," she said, hesitating as if what she said wasn't enough.

"It wasn't your fault. I didn't do it because of you. You tell Barbara he really liked her, but she wasn't the reason."

She did not understand. She stroked his hand and said not to worry about it. The main thing was to get some rest. "And thank God that you are alive. Try to pray," she said. "You need something to hold on to."

She threatened to leave if he did not close his eyes and try to sleep. She continued to hold his hand and talk to him quietly. Eventually he did sleep. She stayed by the bed, fearing that he would wake if she withdrew her hand.

Much later, when he seemed to sense new people in the room, he woke. His grandmother was beside the bed. His eyes blinked, widening a bit more each time until he gained the full sense of who it was. She had been speaking to him already, but the words had not got through.

"What would you like to eat?" she was saying now.

"I'm not hungry."

"You haven't eaten since you've been here. You've got to eat."

"It could have happened to anyone," he said. "You've done things you wish you hadn't done."

"We all make mistakes, Lorne. Now don't upset yourself any more."

"Everyone has to find out for themselves. You can't just play it safe all the time."

From the background a figure stepped into Lorne's

line of vision. Ryan's face looked down at his. It startled him.

"Take it easy, Lorne. Your grandmother'll get the nurse."

"No," he said.

He stared at Ryan's face. Now he cried.

"Leave him alone," he could hear Ryan say. "He has to let it out."

"No!" Lorne bellowed, his eyes closed. "You weren't right. We did what was right! It was our way of doing it."

They rang for the nurse.

Thirty-four

A photograph of the car being hoisted up from the water was on page three. The accident had become news. Lorne insisted on looking at the picture when he saw that his father was trying to keep it from him. He stared at it and saw that it lied. It could show nothing of what had happened. The photographer had taken someone's misfortune and blown it into a warning. It had been generalized into an illustration. Lorne closed the newspaper with certain purpose.

They sat together, the three of them, at the supper table.

"I think I'll go check out the summer job situation tomorrow," he said when he'd finished eating.

"The doctor said you should rest until Monday," his mother remarked quietly.

"If you want to," his father said, "I can't see any reason not to."

There was nothing more said about it. When he left the table to sit in the living room near the window, his father came in carrying something in his hand.

"It's your camera. I carried it into the photo shop in Bakerton. They had it cleaned. They said it might be okay to use again. But they couldn't promise anything."

He passed it to him. Lorne put it in his lap, not bothering to open the case as his father obviously expected him to do.

His father sat on the chesterfield, as near to him as he could get. "And if it's not, perhaps we'll see about getting another one."

"That's okay," Lorne said. "Turn on the TV if you want."

Lorne left the house before dark. He headed to the section of beach that lay under Puffin Head. He sat on the hard beach rocks and looked out at the open water beyond the cove.

A small flat-bottomed boat rested on shore farther along. Its oars lay along the bottom of the boat. He turned it around. Then, pushing from the stern, he gradually moved it toward the water till the bow was afloat.

He walked into the water in his Nikes. He pushed off from shore and jumped aboard all in one motion. With awkward strokes he maneuvered the boat through the shallow part to where the color of the water darkened to its deepest black.

He set the oars inside the boat. He stood up. He loosened the strap from around his neck and passed it over his head. Holding the camera in his hand, he drew back, and with all the power in his body, he flung it to where the land contracted and the open stretch of saltwater continued all the way to France.

Thirty-five

For Elaine's birthday he bought a card. The drawing on the front showed a section of beach with a pair of thin-legged birds approaching it. He thought a long time about the words to fill the blank inside.

In the end he wrote simply, "Happy Birthday, with love," and signed it with the initial of his first name. He studied it and went back to read it many times before sealing the envelope.

When he gave it to her together with the record and the paperback book of poetry, they were in the living room of her house. They sat side by side on the couch as she opened it, taking care not to rip the paper. He searched for distractions around the room. When she finally had it unwrapped, she said that she really liked it, that it was wonderful.

He went with her family for supper on the beach that evening. They drove in the car as close as they could get to the fishing shack where they were to meet her grandfather.

Outside the shack, in a plastic bucket in the shade, were a dozen lobsters, part of her grandfather's catch that morning. Darren, Elaine's young brother, lifted away the seaweed that covered them and poked one with his finger. When it moved, he drew back his finger as fast as he could.

"Take it out," his father told him. "It won't hurt you. Pop got elastic bands on their claws."

He approached it again, cautiously. His hand gripped the back for a second, then drew away.

"Go on," his father said.

He made another try. This time he held on and lifted the lobster away from the rest, raising it above the bucket. Its tail stretched out stiffly and the thin legs on its underside wriggled loose. With newfound confidence he darted the lobster toward Elaine. She jumped back, more out of surprise than fright. He dropped it back in the bucket and hid behind his father before she had recovered enough to yell at him.

Her grandfather emerged from inside, his bulky frame nearly filling the open doorway. Darren wriggled past him under his arm.

"Happy birthday," he said cheerfully.

"And where's my birthday kiss?" Elaine asked.

"Come here, then."

When she approached, he embraced her tightly and planted a firm kiss on her cheek.

They sat around the fire, and the old man, as he no doubt had done hundreds of times before, tossed the lobsters one by one into the froth of the boiling seawater. Within seconds their green color had changed to a bright red.

"Give them twenty minutes from the time they starts to boil again," he said.

When the time had elapsed, Elaine's father tested one to make sure they were cooked. With a stick he fished it up out of the water far enough to get hold of one of the legs. He held it up and gave it a quick jerk. The rest of the body broke away, a sign that they were ready.

Then with Lorne's help he carefully removed the boiler from over the fire and, using a flat piece of board to keep the lobsters from slipping out, slowly drained the water from it onto the sand. He placed the boiler near the slab of bare rock that was to be the dinner table. The old man withdrew the steaming lobsters with his bare hand and tossed them into a heap on the rock.

Anxious to get started, Darren gingerly pulled a lobster toward him from the pile. He let it cool a bit, then broke the claw away from the joint by forcing it against the rock. He sucked the hot juice out from the open end, then started to bang the claw against the rock in an attempt to crack the shell.

"Whaddaya at, old man?" his grandfather said. "Here, come over here, I shows you what to do."

With the claw in one hand and the knife he used for splitting fish in the other, his grandfather demonstrated a quick and easy way to open the shell. He held the claw on edge against the rock and made a short slash downward with the knife so that the blade sank halfway through the shell. A quick sideways twist of the knife, and the shell split cleanly and evenly. The end of the claw meat lay open to view, ready to be slipped out and eaten.

"Now you try it," he said. He handed Darren the knife and a claw from his own lobster.

"Darren, be careful with that knife," his mother warned.

He went through the procedure his grandfather had shown him. On his second try the blade penetrated the shell deeply enough. He broke the end of it away neatly with a turn of the knife.

"There," he said, well satisfied.

Lorne had observed the entire process with intense interest.

The old man eyed him. "He got the hang of it."

Lorne smiled in agreement. The smile caught Elaine's attention. They stared pleasantly into each other's face.

When the two of them had finished eating, they went for a walk along the beach until they were out of sight of the family.

Elaine slipped her hand into his and squeezed it. "You're feeling better," she said.

He stopped, put his arm around her shoulder, and drew her to him as tightly as he could. He was lost in the scent of her close to him.

When his eyes opened it was the roughened expanse of saltwater that filled his view. The wind swept the saltwater toward him.

He loosened his embrace, a sign for her to do the same. He held her hand again, and they continued to walk.

He increased his pace, walking faster, now running, Elaine laughing. His stride stretched their arms until she could keep up no longer and their fingertips broke away from each other. Lorne sprinted ahead, alone.

Thirty-six

At nineteen
he burst out from university
to board a ship across the ocean
to see the Van Goghs in Paris
He broke free—running, panting—
to meet himself along the Seine.

He's gone to make his picture too
It's his own life
to do with what he must do
"Press the button," they said, "we'll do the rest."
But "if only" is a lonely portrait nonetheless
at sixty-five.